Darkness Rising I
Night's Soft Pains

Ed. L. H. Maynard & M. P. N. Sims

Darkness Rising I
Night's Soft Pains

Ed. L. H. Maynard & M. P. N. Sims

Cosmos Books, an imprint of Wildside Press
New Jersey . New York . California . Ohio

Darkness Rising: Night's Soft Pains

Published by:

Cosmos Books, an imprint of Wildside Press
P.O. Box 45, Gillette, NJ 07933-0045
www.wildsidepress.com

For more information, contact Wildside Press.

ISBN: 1-58715-406-4

CONTENTS

Introduction

By HUGH LAMB

The 1930s were golden days for horror anthologies. There was the NOT AT NIGHT series, the CREEPS series, the various bumper books issued by Odhams, John Gawsworth's erratic collections, and the Hutchinson series A CENTURY OF... of which an honorary member must be THE EVENING STANDARD BOOK OF STRANGE STORIES. Published by Hutchinson in October 1934, this massive 1020 page collection, issued anonymously but possibly edited by F.L, Marsh, contained stories that had appeared in the Evening Standard (there was a follow-up volume in 1937 but it was of lesser quality), The list of authors included is impressive, containing as it does names such as E.F. Benson, John Metcalfe, A.M. Burrage, Edith Nesbit, Ambrose Bierce, Algernon Blackwood and Oliver Onions. It should be on every collector's shelf, 'Marriott's Monkey' is a surprisingly unreprinted story from the book, by an author who remains a mystery. All I can say with certainty about him is that he is *not* the 1980s pop star of the same name.

Hugh Lamb, Sutton, Surrey, England, 2001.

Marriott's Monkey

Howard Jones

I must get this down before my reason goes. There is not much time. The pen keeps slipping from my fingers, and my eyes turning to the silver witch-bowl hanging in the window. It is a pretty thing, that witch-bowl. It fascinates me. But it has nothing to do with this story. I must write fast.

It's all about Marriott and his damned monkey. At least, nearly all. Perhaps you recall the name – the Edward Spencer Marriott, who produced a standard work on African mammalia before he was thirty, and whose address to the Royal Society on Mankind's affinity with the apes shocked alike the preachers and the scientific pundits.

To see him you'd never have credited him with brains. He was a hulk of a fellow, standing six foot two in his socks, with a hard, square jaw, and green, childish eyes. At college they called him "The Yokel" because of his simplicity and tenderness – and perhaps out of envy too. The sight of an animal in pain was a physical hurt in him, and because of it he gave himself to the study of things dumb, and helpless. Intellectually none of us was in his class. He was a genius, a giant amongst pygmies. I think it was because I had a better understanding of his shy, soft nature than most men that we became close friends. We passed through and qualified together, Marriott's name at the top of the list, and mine somewhere towards the bottom.

Not long after he came down Marriott went to Africa to collect material for his book. My game was horses, and I moved to Epsom to be near the racing stables. After eighteen months Marriott returned to England, but went abroad again as soon as his book was published. This time he was away six months. When he returned he brought the monkey with him.

He told me all about it one day over lunch in a Bloomsbury restaurant. It was a young male, but I forget now to what particular species it belonged. My memory has gone all to pieces in the past few weeks. It doesn't matter, anyway. Marriott had bought the monkey for ten pounds from the skipper of a cargo boat at Lagos. He believed it was a very good bargain.

"I don't know what made me buy Moka," he said, in answer to one of my questions. "I just felt I had to have him, if you understand. He's a fine chap, tame as you please. You must drop in one evening during the week and see him for yourself."

When I first saw the monkey a few days later I was amused. Marriott was carrying it on his shoulders, pick-a-back fashion, and running up and down his strip of garden, excited as a schoolboy. At the sound of my voice he turned, and over his left shoulder I saw the animal's mouth pressed, as though in affection against the carotid artery in his neck.

"Hey, Moka," he said, with a rather self-conscious laugh. "Meet a new friend." And unclasping the monkey's fingers from his collar, he lifted it into my arms.

It rested there, docile and motionless, for all the world as though it were asleep. I could tell by the hardness of the thigh muscles, and the gleaming softness of its coat that it was in beautiful condition. It raised its upper lip. The teeth were white and clenched. I don't pretend to know much about monkeys, but those clenched jaws seemed... well, peculiar.

As I drew my fingers from its mouth the monkey slowly opened its eyes. Those eyes! Such hatred and malevolence was in them that for some seconds I could only stare back, letting the evil of their look go icily through and through me. Then warmth came into me, and instinctively I pushed the monkey from me. It dropped lightly to the lawn, and curving an elbow on Marriott's leg, slobbered like a sorry child against his knee. Crouching there on the grass, it was a picture of innocence and affection; yet somehow I could not escape the conviction that it was trying to fool me. Almost as if to confirm my thought, it twisted suddenly, and moved swiftly on curved knuckles down the garden to where a blue Persian cat was preening itself in a patch of sunlight. "Here, Moka, come here!" called Marriott, sharply.

The cat stood rigid with arched back and thickened tail. At my friend's command the monkey paused doubtfully, then turned, and slowly lumbered back.

"Poor Peter " said Marriott. "Moka would shake the life out of him if I gave him half a chance!"

"Poor Peter," I said.

We turned into the house, the monkey at our heels. Marriott busied himself with a decanter and siphon, and placed a drink at my elbow.

"What made you drop Moka the way you did?" he asked, settling himself in a chair.

I glanced down to where the monkey was tossing a big rubber ball over its head, catching it with his feet, and throwing it up again.

"I think I must be on Peter's side," I answered, with a grin.

"Oh, you needn't worry about the cat," said Marriott. "Moka's with me most of the daytime, and at night, during this warm weather, I lock him in the shed at the bottom of the garden. Peter sleeps in my room. He's privileged, you see." To the monkey, he said: "Now, Moka, go and shake hands like a gentleman."

The animal's intelligence really was bewildering. It shambled across the carpet, and stretched out a limp and leathery hand. I gripped it, and dropped it, and avoided the artful, upward flash of its dark eyes.

I shall have to rest my hand at this point. It's so awkward to hold the pen, and continual writing gives me the most damnable cramp... Yes, that's better now. That witch-bowl glistens beautifully in the summer sunlight. Where was I? Oh, yes...

An outbreak of coughing in Lord Henry Piggot's stables took me unexpectedly to Newmarket, and a month passed before I visited Marriott again.

I was aware of a subtle yet distinct change in him. His eyes had lost their alertness to a glaze of infinite exhaustion. His shoulders were slightly curved, his head set more closely upon them. When he walked, his arms dangled listlessly, with a curious suggestion of length, and his knees sagged as if the effort of movement were too much for them. The general impression I received was not exactly that of old age, but of a physical crumpling – as if some swift and terrible disease had sapped the vital essences of his body. I wondered if he had been overworking, and asked him (off-handedly, I hoped) how his work of classifying the African languria was progressing.

He answered in a strained and throaty voice: "Haven't touched it, not for a fortnight. Can't settle to work. Touch of nerves. You know how it is sometimes. Let's have a drink, shall we?"

As he turned to lead the way into the lounge, I noticed a small oval-shaped weal on the left side of his neck, set dead across the carotid artery.

"I see you still nurse Moka," I remarked.

"Why... yes, yes," he returned, testily. "Habit of his, kissing me there... Peculiar beast ... affectionate."

At that moment the monkey stirred in a corner of the room, and crossing the floor, climbed into Marriott's chair. It sat there with drooping arms, its eyes closed in an expression of utter lethargy. Something unusual in its appearance impelled me to approach it; and I saw the hair above its temples was flecked with grey. It made no movement until I raised its lip, and then it swung its head away, and set up a beastly, chattering scream.

But I had seen its teeth – and they were yellow. There was no doubt about it. The monkey was ageing fast.

Marriott turned from the sideboard, and murmured caressingly: "There, Moka, there!" He lifted the monkey, and sitting down, set it on his knees, where it rested like some ungainly, sleepy baby. In that same moment he looked towards me, and I swear that beneath the dead expression of his eyes he signalled me an appeal for help.

I was certain then that something dreadful was happening in the house, something beyond all understanding. I was certain, too, that the monkey was at the bottom of it.

"The drinks – there on the sideboard," said Marriott quickly, as though to cover a lapse. "You might... might give me mine." As he took his tumbler from me, I all but cried out. For he grasped it with his palm and his fingers, with his thumb, stuck out awkwardly and uncontrolled, just as a monkey would.

I said, when I had drained my glass: "You need a holiday, Marriott. Try a sea trip, or Majorca for a couple of months. Anywhere to get away from London."

"What about Moka?" he asked, sullenly.

"Send him to a dealer," I suggested. "Or the Zoo might be glad..."

He jumped up, and the monkey swung round his body, and pressed its mouth to his neck.

"You hate him, don't you?" he cried angrily. "Yes, it, you hate him! Want me to get rid of him, don't you?" He paused, sat, and then added with better composure: "Sorry, old man. ... Didn't mean anything. I don't want to go away. Just want to stop here. That's all."

Later that evening, after we had locked the monkey in its shed for the night, I broached the subject again.

"For the sake of your friends, if not for your own sake, you ought to go away," I urged; and something soft and purring rubbed against my leg.

Looking down, Marriott answered: "That dam' cat's fond of you! No, I shan't go away, don't want to.... Dam' cat!"

When I telephoned Marriott three days later to tell him my flat was being redecorated, and that I wanted him to put me up until the work was finished, he knew I was lying. That much was obvious from his suspicious, disjointed haggling. He did not want me – and both of us knew why. But eventually my determination overcame him, and he begrudgingly agreed. I heard him replace the receiver in its hook at the third attempt.

In the following fortnight there were many times when I regretted the impulse of friendship that had sent me to Marriott's side. I had no plans, only a sort of vague hope that somehow my presence would bring him back to normal. But before long I was forced to the conclusion that I served only to bind him and his devilish monkey to a closer relationship. Except at night they were inseparable; and the filthy weal on Marriott's neck grew more and more pronounced as each day passed.

It was terrible to hear his voice becoming shriller and shriller in pitch; to see him playing with the ball, and fumbling with his knife and fork at meal times like a clumsy child; to come across him padding barefooted from room to room, with the monkey clamped to his back. On the first day of my stay with him I lured him from the house on the pretext of exercise, but after half a mile he complained of pain in his dorsal muscles, and only by leaning forward, so that his fingers reached to his knees, could he get relief.

After that he adopted a clumsy cunning to avoid me. One morning I saw him pass through the front door, as if bent on an errand. Less than a minute later there was a scuffling in the garden, and he jumped down from an eight-foot wall with the agility of... well, a monkey. For a few yards he crept in the shadow of some laurel bushes, then made a dash to the door of the monkey's shed. When he found this ruse failed he took to locking himself with the monkey in his bedroom, in the bathroom, and even in the, cellars. His appearance at this time was really shocking, for apart from the increasing emphasis of a withering physique, he found it impossible to shave, or to knot his tie and shoe laces.

Two things in that fortnight saved my sanity. One was the friendliness of Peter, the cat. The other the amazing physical changes in the monkey. It aged beyond belief, as though in pouring out its spiritual self, it had induced a swift decay of the physical body. Eventually it lacked even the strength to fasten its fingers on Marriott's shoulders, so that he was forced to support it by placing his hands beneath its buttocks. Its eyes became jaundiced, and the hatred they had once shown me was replaced by a sort of languid tolerance.

If only the thing would die, I thought – and cursed myself for not thinking of it before.

We locked it in the shed that night at ten. Marriott went off without a word, and I was heartily glad to see the back of him. The vivid weal on his neck was making me feel sick. The cat, according to its custom, followed him upstairs. For two hours I sat alone in the lounge, smoking my pipe and drinking. Then I went into the hall, and took from the wall a knobkerrie Marriott had picked up on one of his tropical visits.

The monkey was hunched in a corner of the shed. In the dim light its eyes seemed triumphantly alive. I swung the knobkerrie, and it was soon over. At the second blow the skull cracked. At the third it shattered.

I washed the knobkerrie under the kitchen tap. As I was replacing it on the hook in the hall there reached me from above a sharp, single scream of feline agony... I took the stairs three at a time – but deep within me there was already the conviction that I was beaten.

The cat lay just beneath the bed, its tongue lolling, its eyes wide and glazed. And Marriott's horrible metamorphosis was complete. He was in the centre of the room, stark naked, his body hooped, and resting on bent fingers. I had time to see that his eyebrows had sunk to a single line, that his nostrils were flattened and dilated, before he sprang at me. He dragged me to the ground, bit at my face, my neck, clawed at my shoulders with his hands, at my legs with his feet. I fought with the strength of ten, with strength born of primeval fear... And, somehow, I was outside tile room, and he was screeching and chattering on the other side of the door. I turned the key. I fainted.

I have had to rest my hand again, a long, long rest this time. But the strength hasn't come back as it ought to. It's agony to touch the pen. I don't care. The story is all but told. I wish you could see that lovely witch-bowl. I feel I must get my fingers about it. I'll try to write for just five minutes more. It's hurting my brain, this effort, as well as my hand.

In five years I've only visited the thing in Brookfield Asylum once. The doctors call it Marriott, but I know better. They won't believe me when I tell them it's not Marriott, but that damned monkey of his.

They phoned me seven weeks ago to tell me Marriott was dying. He'd become terribly old, they said. Now, listen. I told you Marriott bit at my face and neck, didn't I? Well he got my carotid artery. I'm sure if it now. They took me to a nursing home and cauterised me, and put stitches in. But it was too late. He'd got me.

The thing in Brookfield is dying, and my thumb sticks out awkwardly, and I've grown to hate cats.

And there's that lovely witch-bowl I want to play with.

The Old Mill

Kurt Newton

For Jack Adams, only the beauty of his wife and his six-month old son matched the beauty of the day. The sky arched overhead like a great blue canvas; the grass they picnicked on was a plush green carpet. In the distance, the old mill stood, bracketed by trees, looking out of place in this time, in this world of freeways, computer chips and monthly shuttles into space. The tall grey edifice represented something solid and everlasting — the way Jack hoped his life with Sarah and their son, Benjamin, would be.

"Fly fishing on the Comstock River."

Sarah smiled. "What about it?"

"The only other place more beautiful than this."

Sarah thought for a moment. "Bicycling in Arcadia."

"Yeah, that's good one too." Jack looked at his wife, seeing her with the same eyes as he had six years before when they first started dating.

They had been out for a Sunday drive, exploring the countryside, when they spotted the tower of the old mill poking up through the thick summer tree line. When Jack pulled into the weedy lot, they found a grassy embankment topped by a large sprawling oak, the perfect place to spread a blanket and have their lunch. Jack was surprised to see no one taking advantage of such an idyllic spot.

"Want to check out what's inside?"

"But Benny's still asleep."

"Let's bring him. He won't wake up."

Sarah agreed, a bit of the adventurer in her surfacing. They walked down to the mill and looked for a place to enter.

The old mill was once part of a network of thread mills that contributed to making New England the Thread Capital of the World. Now it was nothing more than an empty shell — empty but for a litter of papers strewn about the floor, the mildewed remains of age-warped furniture, and nests of long wooden thread bobbins scattered in piles about the debris. It was like stepping back in time.

"Hey, Sarah, check this one out." Jack held up a yellowed punch card. "George Pickman. He put in 57 hours the week of April 27, 1922. Total pay: $27.36. Damn workaholic. Back then, I bet the guy was rolling in it."

"How about these?" Sarah held up two of the foot-long wooden bobbins. "These would make nice decorator... something-or-others." She frowned. "Maybe lamps for Benny's room?"

Jack ventured deeper into the mill, into a large open space that was once the production area. The walls and floors still held the metalwork of machine mounts. Shallow pools of rusty water and green-tinged sludge provided an obstacle course of slippery footing. There were catwalks overhead, but the stairs leading up to them had been removed. Tall, thin windows, filmed by years of dust and weather, let in a diffused light. Wherever the light touched tiny islands grew — mostly moss and some kind of reddish fungus, soft and gelatinous. Jack picked through some scrap metal, found a nice turn-of-the-century thread machine identification plate. A noise in the corner made him look up. He realized there were probably rats or some nasty-sized spiders lurking about, so he made his way back to the dryer office section to show Sarah his find.

When he returned, Sarah was frantic.

"Jack, you didn't take Benny, did you?"

"No, he's right over —"

Jack's voice caught in his throat. The porta-cradle was where they had left it, in the warm sun that was streaming in through one of the windowless openings. Only now it was empty.

"Sarah. Where's Benny?"

Sarah stared at him, wordless. Her pupils grew large with fear.

"Is this is some kind of a joke?"

She shook her head. "You're not going to believe me, Jack."

"Believe what? Sarah, what did you do with him?"

"I didn't do anything. He was right here. There was this noise, so I turned around, and..."

"And what? For Christ-sakes, Sarah, what?"

"Shhhh." His wife's eyes darted from side to side; tiny tears began to sprout from their corners. "I saw something." She began to shake uncontrollably.

"What are you talking about? *Benny? Where'd you go, Benny-boy?* C'mon, Sarah, he couldn't have crawled far." Jack got down on his knees and looked underneath the old furniture. He overturned mounds of paper. He checked every corner of the room. "Did you look outside?" he asked his wife.

"Benny can't crawl, Jack, you know that."

Jack grabbed his wife and pushed her toward the entrance. "Of course he crawled away. Don't just stand there. Help me look for him!"

They checked outside. Not a mark or a footprint or a tire track. No sign of a silent intruder. Jack went back inside the mill and conducted a more thorough search. Nothing. Not a goddamned thing. It was as if Benny had simply vanished.

How could this happen?

Jack felt the panic closing in, crushing him.

In a fit of frustration, he threw a chair against one of the walls. The wall caved-in as if made of crepe paper, revealing a network of fist-sized channels running through the lathing. Jack heard movements, a scrabbling of claws retreating into the hidden labyrinth.

No.

He hadn't noticed it before, but the old thread bobbins seemed oddly arranged, as if they had been stacked into cone-shaped piles. There was one in each corner of the room, and one larger one in the center, near to where Benny's porta-cradle had been sitting.

Jack kicked at the central pile. The bobbins scattered. Several layers down, the bobbins held their positions, secured in place by a sticky yellow substance. That's when Jack saw the hole. It was worn with age. However, fresh tufts of brown fur were snagged on its splintered edges. The hole was large enough, thought Jack, as he swallowed back dust and fear and his future happiness, for his son to have been dragged down through it.

Outside, Sarah's voice called desperately for their son

...go away...

"Huh?" Jack looked down, but the voice was as if it were coming from inside his own head.

...he is ours now...now go away...

Jack leaned over the gap in the floor. Yellow eyes suddenly appeared within the blackness of the hole.

Jack lurched back, stumbling over a mound of papers. His heart hammered in his chest. He retreated outside into the daylight, to his wife, away from this waking nightmare that had only just begun.

They sat in the car staring at the old mill as darkness settled in. Contacting the police was out of the question. They would be just another headline on the local news. *Couple being held in the disappearance of their infant son. Details at eleven.* Who would believe them?

"Let's go, Jack, we have to get out of here."

"Don't you understand? We can't just leave. It spoke to me, Sarah. Something in there has our son. He could still be alive."

His wife hugged him as if she would never let go. "Jack, if you go back in there, it could get you too."

"I know," he said. "But I won't let that happen." Jack held her tight, wishing for all it was worth that they had never seen the old mill poking up through the trees like a beacon...

...like a beacon drawing them to shore onto the rocks of despair, thought Jack.

As night fell, all was quiet. Strangely, no insect or animal noises accompanied the blanket of stars that appeared overhead. Jack began to doze. He was awakened some time later by a baby's faint cry. Jack could see lights floating behind the rusted windowpanes of the empty mill, alternating from yellow to blue to red. Jack sat in tears, as the infant's cries intensified. "I'm coming for you, Benny," he whispered. "Just hang on."

Thankfully, Sarah was asleep.

But as Jack dozed off for the final time that night, he wasn't sure what he had actually heard or seen, because the summer air was now silent and still, the old mill now dark, its windows illuminated only by the light of the full moon.

With morning came the cold realization of an empty space in their lives. Jack went straight to his trunk. He carried his fishing gear with him wherever he went. He donned his wading boots and brandished a tire iron. He told Sarah to stay behind, go for help if he didn't come back. Sarah grabbed his hand before he left. She smiled weakly.

"I'll get him back," he told her, and kissed her gently on the forehead.

Once again Jack entered the old mill.

The office room was as he had left it, although the central bobbin mound had been carefully rebuilt. He made his way into the open production area. Morning light streamed in through the tall industrial windows, casting a church-like display of dust mote-filled sunbeams.

He listened for sounds. And heard only the silence of the morning.

He called for his son. And still nothing.

He tried to fathom where and for what purpose his son had been taken. The conclusions he reached were all too horribly unreal and unimaginable.

Benjamin?

His toe hit a rise in the floor and he nearly fell forward. A closer inspection revealed a square of plywood nailed in place. There were other squares at regular intervals along the surface of the floor. Jack used the tire iron and pried one of the four-by-four foot covers free. An even rectangle was cut in the wood blocks beneath it — openings once used to allow the belt drives that ran from the motors mounted in a room below to the thread machines that once occupied the production area.

Jack discovered a recess in the wall in the far darkest corner. The opening led to a set of stairs that cascaded down into a sea of darkness. Before descending, Jack used the tire iron and pried the remaining plywood covers off, creating a dozen skylights in the floor. Then, cautiously, he descended the stairs.

The stairway walls were slick with moisture. It was awkward walking on dry land in his wading boots, but the rubber soles gripped the slick cement stairs as if it were an algae-covered river stone. Jack's heart beat heavily in his chest. Amid the drip of condensation and the echo of his footsteps, he could hear faint subterranean movements, perhaps just beneath his feet, shadowing his every move. When he stepped off the last stair onto the sub-room floor, the sounds suddenly ceased.

Pools of total darkness ran concurrent with the spots of sunlight beaming in from above. At first, Jack thought the mill had left their machine motors behind. He realized quickly the objects he saw standing amid the wide open floor space were mounds of dirt and stone piled high into cones. He made his way to the center of the room and stood beside one of the mounds, which was half-illuminated by the light from above. "I want him back!" he shouted.

The eyes appeared in sets of two, the blackness suddenly filling with a dozen tiny yellow reflectors. Then two dozen. Then fifty. Then a hundred, and more. They drew toward him. As some of the creatures crossed into the light, Jack could see he wasn't dealing with rats at all, or feline strays, or any other recognizable creatures, although they had features reminiscent of many animals common to the region. Some had large cat-like eyes and rat-tails. Others bore wings like those of a bat and yet crawled on all fours like an opossum. Others displayed miniature antlers. It was as if they couldn't decide which animal form they liked best.

Jack raised the tire iron and the creatures hesitated. He lowered the bar and they began to converge. He raised it again. They halted. "It's these cones of yours, isn't it?" Jack feigned like he was going to smash the dirt structure. A nervous whistling rose from the surrounding brood. "I wonder what's so precious about them?" he asked rhetorically. "Ah, what the hell..." He swung the tire iron and connected with the cone's outer surface.

The blow crumbled half the structure in a spray of dirt and gravel. To Jack's horror, inside the cone sat the face of a stranger. Below the neck, the body was missing. The head was mounted on a mushroom-like stalk that glowed with a cobalt blue light.

The face opened its eyes and stared at Jack. It mouthed the words "Help me."

Revulsed, Jack plunged his tire iron into the face's forehead. The neck-stem snapped and the face collapsed in on itself and bled into a pool of greenish-blue slag.

The whistling noises from the surrounding creatures rose higher. Jack moved onto the next mound. The brood converged, nipping at his ankles, clawing at the thick rubber material of the wading boots. Jack smashed the next cone. And the next. Inside each one was a human head, the remains of hitchhikers perhaps, transients — the mill had probably looked like a safe place to camp for the night — each one alive in some inexplicable way. Relief spread across each face as Jack wielded his tire iron and released them from their torment.

As the last cone was shattered, Jack discovered his son was not among them.

By now, the creatures were frenzied, they clamored atop each other to get at him. It was getting difficult for Jack to walk, like wading through a fast-running rapid. Jack beat at the distorted animals and they hissed, squealed and chattered. But they didn't stop coming. They had him cornered.

"Over here! Hey!"

Jack turned to see Sarah standing on the stairway, a halo of bright red light surrounding her like a sunset-lit Madonna. She waved a road flare at the swarm of creatures as she stepped down into the sub-room. The creatures turned to face her.

"Glad you could make it," said Jack.

Sarah moved closer, pushing the creatures back, but she suddenly stopped. She stared past Jack and nearly dropped the flare. She pointed. "Jack, look."

Along the back wall, cast in the reddish glow of the road flare, they had found what they had come looking for.

A gelatinous mass was spread across the entire surface of the sub-room's wall. It moved with a slow, deliberate undulation. Strangely colored lights coursed through the surface of its skin. *It was alive.* There was the suggestion of a head; several eye-like keyholes. And cradled in its central mouth-like orifice, lay their son, Benny.

The infant giggled as if riding a play horse. His tiny hands reached up as a thin strand of goo descended from the maw and bobbed like a crib toy.

Sarah screamed, "He is not your child!"

The sentient beast whispered into their brains, *You were all my children once...but you have chosen to live apart....*

Jack felt a wave of sadness overcome him, an ancient tug of what might have been. He felt himself drawn toward the beast, hypnotized by its color and movement. It reminded him of fishing...the lazy rippling movements of the water as everything is carried downstream....

His legs carried him closer. Benny looked so happy, so content.

"Jack, no!"

Slippery tendrils slithered toward him.

And just as Jack was about to offer himself to the great fungal beast mother, Sarah's pleas broke through his drowning consciousness. Jack looked up into the beast's ill-defined face. "I can't let you take him," he shouted, and quickly grabbed Benny from the gelatinous maw.

But he didn't get far. Benny's umbilical cord had regrown. The accordion-like attachment wound down inside the maw, now connected to the beast.

The beast laughed. *He has made his choice*, it whispered hideously, *it is time you make yours.* Tendrils wrapped around Jack's feet and snaked up his legs.

Jack could think of only one thing to do -- the way primitive man must have freed himself from the whims and wills of Nature's callousness. Jack opened his own mouth and bit the umbilical cord with his teeth.

His son cried out as a spray of yellow fluid exited the cord. A groan followed from deep within the sub-room floor. Jack unhooked his suspenders and let the wading pants fall. He stepped free of the pants as the tendrils dragged them away.

"Now, Sarah, now!" he yelled, and Sarah threw the still-burning road flare at the beast mother's weeping maw, where it stuck like a wick in candlewax.

The beast mother's colors deepened to an angry violet. Her colors raced. She began to swell.

"Let's get out of here!" Jack shouted as he handed Benny over to Sarah. He pointed toward one of the openings above.

He fought off the swarm of lesser creatures as best he could as he hoisted Sarah up and out of the sub-room, where she crawled to safety. Finally, it was his turn. He leaped up and hung by the lip of the opening.

But the topside surface was slick with sludge. His grip was slipping. Some of the creatures had latched onto his pantlegs and were gnawing through into his ankles. The smell of burning vegetable matter was in the air. Fire had spread along the surface of the fungal wall. The beast mother's howl was a deafening shriek inside his skull.

Jack felt his fingers sliding. "Sarah!" he yelled and hands grabbed hold of his arm. With a grunt, Sarah pulled him up out of the spreading inferno.

But their relief was short-lived. The swarm of creatures swelled up the stairway. Jack thought this was it, they would die this way, chewed apart in one last orgiastic fit of triumph. The beast mother would claim them after all.

But no. The creatures ran in differing directions, scattering like leaves in the wind to the outer reaches of the factory, finally released from their stewardship. A thick black smoke followed their exodus, spewing from the stairwell and the dozen openings in the woodblock floor.

Jack and Sarah got to their feet. With Benny cradled between them, they too ran for the exit.

Once clear, they stood in silence and watched the old mill burn. Amid the cracks and snaps, they also heard what sounded like screams and whispers rising up out of the flames. But perhaps they were only hearing the remnants of ancestral voices now singed from their memory.

As near as Sarah could tell, there was nothing wrong with Benny. She tied his umbilical cord off with a tightly wound rubberband. Already Benny's distended navel was beginning to desiccate, the yellow fluid turning to a phosphorescent powder.

"Let's go home," Jack said.

And as the first of the fire sirens sounded in the distance, they pulled out of the weedy lot, away from the idyllic and into the mundane, and tried to forget that the past two day's events had ever happened.

The following day the papers reported that the hundred-year old mill had burned to the ground. Town authorities had long wanted to sell the property, the article said, but it seemed there was no one willing to buy the old mill, which the locals claimed was haunted by strange lights, and was even blamed for several disappearances in the area.

Months later, these same reports began to surface about the home of Jack and Sarah Adams, who were found murdered — beheaded, in some strange ritual sacrifice — their bodies never found, their year-old infant son abducted and still missing.

The house stands vacant, a For Sale mounted on the lawn.

At night, neighbors say they see strange lights in the windows that alternate from yellow to blue to red.

Beggar and Child

Walt Jarvis

It was disgraceful, Mr. Davenport thought, his hand tightening on the overhead stirrup, that the authorities didn't do something about the beggar woman. He was sure that there were laws in Italy that addressed such gross mendicancy, but they obviously weren't being enforced on the Milan Red Line. The best thing for him, a foreigner, to do was to look away and pretend he didn't see her.

Every day, at the same time it seemed, she appeared in his subway car. Mr. Davenport did not know if she got on at Piazza de Angeli, the previous stop, or much earlier, and it just took her awhile to work her way back. Here she was again, slowly forcing her way through the crowd of commuters, a battered tin cup held in one hand, the other cradling a baby wrapped in dirty rags, begging, no, demanding lira from the passengers in a harsh, sing-song voice.

It did not appear to bother the Italians as much as it did him. The middle-aged man with the profile of a Roman senator kept his eyes locked on his newspaper, shaking his head with a frown when the beggar held the tin cup almost under his patrician nose, but never deigning to look at her. A young couple, the girl a striking Venetian blonde, continued to embrace and whisper to each other as the woman sidled by, her voice rising in a screech as if she begrudged them their adolescent bliss.

Then she bore down on Mr. Davenport. He turned his eyes toward the window so he wouldn't have to look at her, watching instead the ochre-colored walls of the subway tunnel plunge into darkness as the train left the stop. Unexpectedly the car pitched hard to the right, throwing him against her. He was horrified to hear a thump and a kind of muffled cry, and looking down, saw the beggar woman sitting on her rear at his feet, the child resting at a cock-eyed angle across her bony chest.

Filled with a foreigner's horror of having caused an incident in a strange land, he bent down to help her up. She reared back and hissed at him, baring her teeth. Roughly cradling the baby under her arm, she struggled to her feet. "I'm terribly sorry," Mr. Davenport mumbled, then looked around with an embarrassed smile, as if to say, "It's only half my fault." The reaction from the other passengers was not what he expected: The young couple stared at him accusingly, the patrician in the cashmere coat glared down his nose at Davenport.

The beggar appeared to be in no hurry to move on. She was staring intently at him from one of the metal hand poles that she had latched on to, like some kind of monstrous bird on its perch, her mouth half open, revealing a detonated mine field of blackened teeth. He could not help stealing a glance at the baby. It had not cried out at the fall; it appeared to be sleeping. At least its eyes were shut. Perhaps it was drugged, and that was why it was so still.

Even though the cup was resting at her side, he removed his wallet from his hip pocket and peeled off a 10,000-lira note. "There," he said slipping the ridiculously flimsy money into its dirty interior. With a sound that was a cross between a phlegmy cough and a snarl she pushed the cup at his face again.

"I said I was sorry," he said angrily in English. "That's all you're going to get."

With a surge of relief he saw that his stop was coming up. As the subway car jerked to a halt, he pushed his way past the woman to reach the exit. Davenport felt her hands clawing at him, and he swiveled sharply, sure that she was after his wallet. It sent him boomeranging into a middle-aged dowager wearing too much lipstick and rouge, who squawked in outrage. Inadvertently he had stepped on her foot.

As soon as the door opened with a pneumatic hiss, Davenport shouldered his way through. A phalanx of passengers hurrying to board the car cut him off. He stood helplessly on his tiptoes, barred from moving forward by the swarm. Then they were around and past him, and he saw a clear path to the street. In a few minutes he would be in the safety of his apartment.

Mr. Davenport heard the train start up behind him and looked over his shoulder, hoping to see it carrying the gypsy woman away. Instead he found himself staring into her wrinkled face, her burning black eyes fixed menacingly on him. Burdened by the baby, she took a step after him, moving awkwardly as if she were crippled.

Now he saw her interest in a more sinister light. Was she a member of a gang of gypsies, following him to signal him out to her compatriots, so they could roll him on some dimly lit street, rob him of his wallet, perhaps slit his throat?

He turned away, pretending to ignore her, but found his way blocked by a new wave of commuters rushing to the edge of the platform. Suddenly he felt her fingers clawing at his cashmere coat. Davenport twisted around, instinctively raising his arm to strike out at her. Of course, he had overreacted: she was just trying to get his attention to demand more money. Just as quickly the woman held the baby in front of her as if to ward off a blow.

Their eyes locked together. It was as if he saw her clearly for the first time. The beggar's head was a skull only thinly sheathed with wrinkled, olive-toned flesh. There was a dark hollowness to her cheeks that hinted at tuberculosis or some other debilitating disease. Dirt was so embedded in her skin that it was hard to tell if she were swarthy or simply filthy. Her greasy gray hair disappeared beneath a sweat-stained kerchief. She muttered something at him — whether it was a plea for more lira or a curse he could not tell —and took a step closer.

In the same flash, Mr. Davenport saw how beautiful the child was — dirty, yes, but bearing perfect features beneath a fine cap of jet black hair. Eyes still shut, despite the noise. He remembered the folk tales from his youth that accused the gypsies of stealing babies and wondered momentarily If this child wasn't a testament to those old wives' stories. Surely nothing as loathsome as the old woman could have given birth to such a beautiful child.

"Go away!" Davenport yelled. "Go away and leave me alone!" He only meant to wave her away, but somehow, as if they had a will of their own, his hands made contact and he found them pushing at her. The woman stumbled backwards, a wide-eyed expression of alarm on her face. She teetered on the edge of the platform, trying to regain her balance, but the weight of the child threw her off balance. Davenport reached out for her, but she fell over backwards before he could grab her arm, and into the path of an oncoming train. A squeal of brakes, the ear-shattering blast of a horn, her arms outstretched to give Davenport the baby, then the engine picked them up and tossed them into the air. She bounced against the wall and fell in a heap on the platform, the baby in its blankets landing next to her. It had never cried out, never made any noise at all. Later Davenport tried to convince himself that it had been lifeless all along.

"It is unfortunate that you should have such a tragic experience in our country," Inspector Daneli said. He was a compact man with thinning black hair that was pomaded close to the skull. He wore an exquisitely cut wool suit and an expensive-looking bejeweled watch, which he kept checking from time to time.

He offered Davenport an American cigarette from a gold case.

"No thanks, I don't smoke," Davenport said.

"So much of the crime that blackens the reputation of Milan comes from these people," the inspector said, after lighting a cigarette of his own. "These gypsies — the zingari. You can blame them for the pick pocketing, the petty thefts, the unsightly begging in the streets. They're barely European, you know."

Davenport nodded as if he were already aware of that.

"It was unfortunate that the woman who was harassing you lost her balance and was hit by the train; doubly unfortunate for the child. These people use their infant's cold-bloodedly to squeeze even more money out of the passers-by. Especially foreigners. You must not blame yourself, Mr. Davenport. It was an accident, which would not have occurred had the woman left you alone. Remember that, if you should have any lingering remorse"

That was easy for the inspector to say. He had not been there as the train came sweeping through the tunnel, or seen the look in the woman's eyes as she tried to hand him her baby.

Davenport awoke from his drug-induced stupor and lay staring at the darkened room. The window was open and he could hear the sounds of late-night Milan traffic from the boulevard two blocks away. His bedroom had a high ceiling but was almost claustrophobically narrow, so there was barely enough room for his bed, an armoire and dresser.

He had taken a sleeping pill and a half, a regular ritual since the accident, and that should have put him out for the night. Instead, Mr. Davenport had been awakened by what he thought foggily was a crying child. He lay in his bed, hoping that he had only dreamt it, and then heard it again. It was faint but insistent, and seemed to be coming from the courtyard below his apartment window.

He climbed reluctantly from the high, narrow bed and, his arms folded across his chest, trudged over to the window and looked down. The courtyard was a blue-black well surrounding by frowning red-bricked walls. Most of the people who lived in the surrounding apartments were well past the childbearing age. Davenport did not remember ever seeing a child on the elevator he took to reach the fourth floor. Of course, he told himself, it could have been someone's grandchild, here for a visit, that he heard. He tried to identify the apartment it was coming from, and was disturbed to find that the source seemed to be the courtyard itself. Impossible, he told himself. No one would let a child go outside to roam those damp cobblestones this time of night.

A chilling thought occurred to him: perhaps the baby had fallen from a window of one of the apartments and lay injured and helpless below, while its parents slept on. In his mind's eye Davenport saw the bloody bundle huddled on the concrete platform after the train shuddered to a halt, and fought to blank that image out. The effort left him trembling and drenched with sweat, but when he opened his eyes again the crying had stopped.

As he started to turn away from the window, the faint sign of movement at the bottom caught his attention. Something small and pale was laboriously making its way in a diagonal across the floor of the court-yard. Strain as he might, there was not enough light for Mr. Davenport to make out what it was. It must be an old cat, he told himself; old or badly injured. Just because it looked vaguely like a child crawling on all fours had to be a trick of the light, enhanced by his traumatized imagination working overtime. He was tempted to descend the stairs in the darkness to find out and fought against it. Nothing's down there, Mr. Davenport told himself, clenching and unclenching his fists. If you give into this nightmare, what will be next? Camping out down there in the dark, waiting for an apparition to appear that only exists in your mind? Snuffling about the subway, trying to undo what can never be undone? He lay there in the darkness, his eyes wide open, as time slowly passed, trying to concentrate on the sounds of Milan stirring at the beginning of a new day, praying not to hear, beneath the distant rumbling of traffic and the sleepy voices echoing in the hallway, the muted cry of a child.

For a long time after the accident, Davenport did not take the subway. He would take a cab to the Central Station, and then walk from there. Cab fares were very expensive in Milan, and the aggressive driving of the taxi drivers frightened him immensely. Every day on his way to the cab-stand he passed the entrance to the Metropolitana, but he averted his eyes from that gaping doorway that led to the rushing trains underground. Still, he knew he would have to take it again to prove, if nothing else, that he could do it; that he was in control of his own mental well being.

When that time came, it was as difficult as he had feared. He paused at the top of the steps that led to the entrance, fighting an attack of panic, his nostrils full of the warm, fetid air that escaped from below, a motionless boulder around which surged the torrent of commuters. Reluctantly he descended the steps, edged past the African immigrants selling leather bags and silk ties, along the off-putting ochre-colored walls and through the metal turnstiles and the second set of steps that led to the Red Line below.

Waiting for the train to arrive, he was careful not to look in the direction of the spot where the accident had taken place. Of course, there would be no indication that it had ever happened; the Italian authorities had efficiently seen to that.

He entered a car that did not appear to be too full and turned away from the platform. He could see it reflected in the windowpane, but dimly because of the grime and fingerprints, which Mr. Davenport nonetheless found somehow reassuring. A commotion erupted behind him and he stiffened, remembering that was how the beggar woman had always burst into the car. He looked over his shoulder and saw that it was only a passel of Milanese high-schoolers, the boys acting up to get the attention of their female companions.

Mr. Davenport breathed a ragged sigh of relief; as he turned back to his view of the subway wall he thought he saw a hunched over figure hurrying across the platform, a bundle clutched in its arms. He pushed his way through the other passengers to the opposite side of the car to get a better look, but the train had already swept into the tunnel, and the platform was lost from sight. The image haunted him even after he reached his office near the Pirelli tower. For a long time he sat at his desk, ignoring the blinking phone message light, and the reports his secretary had so carefully arranged for him to peruse, staring into the dreary fall day, and seeing only that bent shape passing in a flash across the platform of the subway station; an image that he continued to see again and again, like a loop of film that shows continuously.

The child's crying continued unabated every night. No matter how many sleeping pills Davenport took, he could not escape it for long. Even when the windows were closed and the drapes pulled, he thought he could hear it, as persistent as the buzzing of a mosquito. Davenport even thought about complaining to the authorities, but, knowing how much most Italians loved children, he imagined what kind of hearing he would get.

He asked his one neighbor that he had a speaking acquaintance with, Signora Gassman, if the noise from the crying child bothered her at all. "Noise? What noise?" she asked. "There are no children in this apartment, Signor, only old people, a few childless couples and single men such as yourself."

Everywhere on the streets he saw beggars. They were lurking under the roofs of the arcades, gathered on the corners of the Corso Buenos Aires, slouched against the walls where the subway corridors intersected, their hands stretched out like claws. Their presence did not seem to bother the sleek, well-dressed Milanese who ignored them as they hurried down the sidewalks, making deals on their cell phones, but their presence weighed heavily on Davenport.

Only one beggar really mattered, though, and he only saw her in his dreams. There always came the moment when she reached out to him with her cup and he drew back. It was that motion that seemed to propel her away from him, over the edge of the platform in slow motion. Mr. Davenport would always awake in a sweat, gasping for breath, his heart beating wildly. When he regained control of himself, it was only to hear in the cold silence of the night the rising wail of the unseen child.

He boarded the Metropolitana at six o'clock, squinting in the bright fluorescent lights that made his eyes ache, wincing at the shaking motion of the car, His head felt as if it were going to explode from a pulsing headache that had lodged like a shard of glass in the center of his brain and was cutting its way deeper and deeper with each jerky start and stop of the car.

Mr. Davenport's only consolation was that it was his last ride. Tomorrow he would begin his vacation; in exactly twenty-five hours he would be back in his native Cleveland, where the only beggars were downtown, a place where Mr. Davenport never went, a place far from the eastern suburb, an orderly haven of rolling lawns and well-planned subdivisions, where he had grown up.

He was desperate to leave his apartment on Via San Agosto, where the distant wailing of the child had become as much as fixture as the 18th-century armoire. Finally he had called the authorities, and, after an appropriate delay, they had come back to him with the pronouncement that there was no child in the building, and that none of his neighbors reported hearing anything.

He was remembering how foolish he had felt, listening to the policeman's report, seeing the skepticism in the other's calm brown eyes while he, Davenport, insisted that there was a child somewhere, there had to be. When he saw the woman at the far end of the car, Mr. Davenport stiffened in terror: it was impossible, he knew very well it was a hallucination, but there she was, her head bowed low so he could not see her face. The face of the baby, however, was clearly visible over her shoulder. Was it the same child? Davenport could not tell; to him all Italian children looked alike.

She was moving away from him toward the opposite end of the car, and Davenport realized that she would be out of his sight in a matter of minutes. He felt he had been given a second chance, to do, finally, what had been left undone. He would give her more money and thereby end his nightmare. As he pushed his way through to the adjoining car, he fumbled in his pocket for his wallet. This time he would give 50,000 lira, 100,000, no, all the money he possessed. He extricated his wallet, always a risky thing to do on the Metropolitana because of pickpockets, looking for the largest lira notes it contained.

The crowded car did not make his passage easy. He murmured, "Scuzi, scuzi," over and over as he forced his way through. A group of schoolchildren in blue and white uniforms tittered at his almost comical haste. Others did not find it so amusing: a low rumble of protest followed in his wake. It was hard enough for people to keep their balance on the moving subway car without being jostled by a massive, clumsy foreigner.

In the meantime, she had made her way into the next car. Davenport hurled himself into the knot of people standing in front of the interconnecting door. Someone cursed him, and he saw a dark, Sicilian-looking face glaring at him threateningly. He had almost forced the door open when the train shuddered to a stop. He groaned with frustration as he saw the beggar woman step onto the platform, but he managed to reach the exit door of his car just before it closed. Still, she had quite a lead. Somehow she managed to keep just ahead of him, snaking up the platform's steps and into the cold night air despite his calling out desperately for her to stop.

On the open street, there were few people to bar his way and he shortened the distance rather quickly. She knew now that she was being followed, for she kept glancing wildly over her shoulder at him. She would have broken into a run, but she was hampered by the weight of the baby.

He didn't want to hurt her; he only wanted to redeem himself. Why couldn't she understand that? She turned down a side street that ended in a barren piece of land that descended to a boggy marsh area that met the river. He saw her join a group of people lounging against the side of one of those little European campers that looked so woefully small in comparison to their American counterparts. A small gas stove cast a reddish glare over their fierce faces. The air was drenched with the smell of garlic.

As he approached them in a half run, the woman said something in a harsh, strident language that was not Italian, and the group gathered around her in a protective cordon. One of the men, short, swarthy looking, muscles bulging under a black leather jacket, started yelling something warningly at Davenport, but he ignored him. He had to get through to her, to tell her he had never meant to hurt anyone. He shouldered his way through, grabbed her by the shoulder and spun her around.

A wild-eyed youngish face, marred with a beaked nose and a bad overbite, looked into his eyes. A beggar woman, but not the beggar who haunted his dreams. As the angry men knocked him down and began kicking at him, cursing him in that harsh, unknown language, Davenport tried to protect his face and stomach. They will not kill me, he thought, because then it will be over. That would be too easy.

Finally they finished with him, and left him lying on the ground, his mouth a bloody wound, his ribs stabbing like knives every time he breathed. For a long time he lay motionless as the moon rose over the distant confectioner's towers of the Duomo, flooding the marshland with a cold, pitiless light. His mind was filled with another kind of clarity as bright in its way as the moonlight. Mr. Davenport understood that this way he would never escape the visions of the beggar woman, or the wailing cry of the child, no matter how far from Milan he fled. Every time he went down a set of stairs he could expect to find her crouched at the bottom. He could not buy his way out of this punishment; no matter how many lira he threw at the streetcorner beggars. His salvation required something else. As the moon grew brighter and brighter, like the headlight of an oncoming train, he was overcome with the realization that his life, the life he knew and was comfortable with, was over. It would be replaced inexorably by something rising out of the darkness like the stench from the slime-covered ground, whose confines he had already glimpsed in the black eyes of the gypsy woman as she had looked up at him just before the train hit, reaching out with the baby in her hands.

Inspector Daneli never took the subway, but today his little gray Lancia was in the shop, so he did not have any choice. He chose a seat that looked reasonably clean and sat down to read his Corriere de la Sera

He heard the beggar coming before he saw him. He tried to ignore the rasping voice calling out for alms, but it was so insistent, and the words uttered in such an odd, unidentifiable accent, that in the end he had to look up.

A figure was advancing down the center of the aisle, wearing a shapeless topcoat that had been of good quality once but which now was badly stained and greasy-looking. A brown knit cap had been pulled low over one brow, giving its wearer an air of grotesque insouciance. The face that peered out from under it was dirty and unshaven, the cheeks covered with a salt-and-pepper beard of several months' cultivation, beneath which festered an ugly-looking red-and-white rash. Several teeth were missing from his mouth.

In one hand the man held an old cup, half filled with lira from other passengers on the train. His other arm cradled an old doll, its plastic face frozen in an open-mouthed smile, its bright blue eyes winking and blinking as he walked.

Inspector Daneli placed a 500-lira note in the receptacle. The man murmured 'Grazie" in an alcohol-laden voice, and, reeking of sweat and urine, shambled on. Daneli followed his disappearing hulk with disapproving eyes. The man looked familiar although Danelli could not place him. He was obviously a foreigner, perhaps an Albanian or a refugee from some other war-torn place in the east. He didn't look like an East European, however. He looked like an American, although that didn't make sense. Americans didn't need to beg in the subways of Milan; they were all too rich.

Then it came to him. He looked uncannily like the American the inspector had questioned a year ago after an accident in the subway. Again, that seemed highly unlikely; that businessman had probably returned, much to his relief, to the United States some time ago.

Inspector Daneli reminded himself to look up the rules on deporting indigent foreigners when he returned to his office at central headquarters. This one would probably be easy enough to track down, given his unusual appearance. Milan had enough of its own beggar riff-raff without becoming a dumping ground for the rest of the world. As the beggar disappeared into the next car, the doll's right eye slid shut in a mechanical wink as if slyly agreeing with him.

Best-Kept Secret

Kim Guilbeau

Suspend your beliefs. Forget what you've been taught.

I'm about to tell you the truth.

It began as an ordinary day, the day I died. No warning came. No tingling of my spine. No dread churning in my stomach. And you know those flashes we're supposed to have? Like flipping through a photo album in your mind... me as a child, graduations, wedding... it never happened. All you see is black.

Snow began to fall early that morning, lightly at first, like a veil of white lace drifting to the earth. The sight of it brought smiles to the weary faces of my co-workers, and as I walked from a meeting back to my office I heard the light humming of a Christmas carol emanating from under one of the closed doors. Later that afternoon, as hours had passed and I found a moment to gaze out my office window, I saw that the snow had transformed the land into camouflaged hills of white. The gray sky was beginning to turn dark and the roads looked treacherous.

I took a quick walk around the office. As usual, everyone was still there. It was a competitive atmosphere and face time was important, so important that Nathaniel and I had put off having a family until our mid-thirties and while I was now close to forty and we'd been trying for four years, it seemed like we were too late.

I left the office early. Maybe the blinding fluorescent lights and the incessant humming of my monitor finally got to me. Maybe it was the voices drifting from the water cooler about stock options, IPO's, and mutual funds. Or maybe it was Angelina, the pregnant secretary, whose cubicle faced my office all day long. All I knew was that I wanted to leave.

I snuck out the back way, leaving my office light and computer on to hide my secret. Even from my office window I could tell that the roads were slick and dangerous. I had devoted much of my whole life to this company, but I wasn't about to die for them.

I drove carefully, keeping a safe distance back from the car in front of me. But we all know that it isn't our driving we should worry most about. I saw the car coming fast in the rear view mirror. Too fast. He was the epitome of an egocentric, self-indulgent pig, speeding through a snowstorm in his all-terrain SUV that could plow through snow banks six-feet thick yet not stop any faster than a VW Bug. He was switching lanes in the dense traffic while placing a call order to his stockbroker on his cell phone.

I saw it happen in slow motion in the mirror. His tires kicking up avalanches of snow as the brakes squealed. The back end twisting to the left as the tires refused to tread on the ice. The look of horror on his face and the cell phone falling through the air from his open hand.

The pig crushed the whole rear end of my Camry. My bumper lay on the side of the road and on-lookers could actually see into my trunk between the twisted metal. Other than a sore neck and an instant bruise on my forehead, I was fine. The pig grumbled and complained about the city's poor snowplowing as we exchanged information. He never even apologized.

When I arrived home, Nathaniel was waiting for me in the entryway with a knife. The curtain was drawn to one side, so I knew he had seen the damage on the car as I parked it. His handsome face was covered with the mask of an angry scowl, but it immediately faded into concern as he saw the bruise on my forehead.

He inquired about the accident, and I informed him first that it was not my fault and filled in the details as I continued. He seemed satisfied with that and the knowledge that the pig's insurance company would most likely cover all the damage. His disposition appeared to be unusually mild and I was glad. I was in no mood for an argument.

He returned to the kitchen to continue slicing vegetables for our dinner. I usually offered to help, but that evening all I wanted was to sink into a hot bath and lose myself in the scent of the foaming bubbles. I needed to heat the sore muscles in my neck and soothe the raging thoughts in my mind.

When the bathtub was full and my body was naked, I slowly slipped one foot into the tub. The water was too hot and my foot immediately turned red and stung with the burn. As I tried to reverse my direction mid-stride, my attempt to retreat from the tub miscarried and my foot slipped. I don't know exactly how my clumsy self managed to do it, but I did it. My head smacked against the side of the tub as my body fell into it and my already sore neck snapped like a dead twig.

And that was it.

I never expected death to come so unextravagantly. I'm not complaining; it was quick and painless. But I always thought that if I died young it would be more heroic or at the very least romantic. But we can't choose how death takes us. He just does.

The next time I experienced sight again, my eyes were living in the tiny stomachs of maggots and other little creatures that lived in the soil with my body. I didn't know how long it had been since I had died, but knew it was some time since the decomposition process was already underway.

The next thing that hit me was utter, blinding confusion. But before I even tried to sort through what was happening the sinking began. I felt myself being physically drawn or pulled deeper into the earth. My initial thought was that some mammoth graveyard creature was taking my body to his den to save me for later, but then I realized that I was sinking but my body wasn't. As I retreated further into the earth's core my body appeared smaller and smaller until I couldn't even see it anymore. That's the last I saw of my physical self, and in its current condition I didn't really want to see it again.

When I reached the center of the core, all the answers came to me. There's no lobby or waiting area. There's no training room, or class where the new rules are taught to you. You just know. It's like an understanding just drifts into your mind and you can't believe that you didn't know it all along. To you... it's like breathing, I suppose.

The first other essence I met was that of my grandfather and I thought that was quite odd at first since he was alive when I died. But as soon as my mind questioned it, the answer came. He beat me there. He was cremated and the trip to the core is faster through that route.

The thing about the essences is that they're pretty much the same as the people were. A grumpy old man in life becomes a grumpy old essence in the core. My grandfather demonstrated this fact immediately with complaints about neighboring essences.

Another funny thing about the core is that the good and the bad people are not separated as everyone expects them to be. But then again, aren't we all somewhat good and bad? The bad people can't hurt you in the core, though. Your body is gone so you feel no pain and can inflict no pain on other essences. Physical pain, that is. Whatever emotional baggage you left with comes with you. The bad people are, in a way, punished for their sins on earth since they seem to have the most emotional problems to deal with in the core.

Some essences try to dig their way back. Some even make it. They roam around the earth, searching for answers from their past or just causing trouble. Most of the time they come back when they feel more at peace. Sometimes they forget who they are... get lost, and never come back.

Those essences are the clichés of the earth's supernatural realm. The cold spots. The feeling of being watched. Movement out of the corner of your eye. Whispers in the dark.

All the ghost stories you hear about... they're real. They're us. It's the best-kept secret.

Investigations

John Shire

"This thick and bloated beauty,
that blooms in the darkest places..."
from 'Fungoids' by Enoch Soames.

"Is it dangerous?"

"I don't know. Do you care?"

In a tiny, airtight glass bottle, a smaller piece of grey fungus. Grof took the offering, looked past the other man at his untidy flat and wondered whether he was ready for another trip. Grof's rooms had seen far better days. Since he had lived there they had decayed even further, well below the level at which any less confused character would have moved out. Grof, however, did not look the kind of man who cared about such things. Thin to the point of emaciation, the filthy jeans and t-shirt that he wore barely found any flesh on which to hang. He had a hunted and haunted look that exposed his obsessive experiments with hallucinogens to perfection.

"Eat it as soon as you open the bottle. The Doctor told me it has a tendency to deliquesce on exposure to air. Take the whole piece. Don't waste time trying to save any, it dissolves phenomenally fast."

The other man looked far healthier by comparison. Shorter by several inches, he looked relaxed even in the repellent surroundings. He had provided Grof with drugs for some time now, building him up to a state of dependence that gave the smaller man an unconscious pleasure. This unpleasant fact showed itself in his face whether he liked it or not. Grof would not, and did not, notice these things anymore.

"Thanks. Here, take the money. I'll try it this afternoon."

"I'll call round later if you want, just to check on you. Unusual stuff you know."

Even Grof noticed this unlikely concern. He looked sharply at Lardner, noticing, perhaps for the first time, how well dressed he was for a hospital orderly. How could he afford such a new leather jacket, the newest haircut, the gold watch? Then the reason occurred to him and he floundered.

"Ok, if you like. Or I'll call you when it's over."

"Hey, yeah, alright. I work in a hospital ok? I treat you like we treat real patients. Don't look so miserable. Remember, have a good time."

He tapped the unlabelled jar before leaving, as if for luck. Grof could swear he was whistling as he strolled down the corridor. Lardner made the money he did from people like Grof. That was how you got on in this world, how you got to wear gold watches. He sat down and sighed. Try not to think too much. Now seemed as good a time as any.

He popped the top off the jar, shook out the lump of fungus and placed it on his tongue, all in one quick movement, well before he had time to consider what he was doing.

For a split second it smelt and tasted so thoroughly revolting that he thought he would throw it straight back up. Gross fumes seemed to rise directly into his brain. Tiny spores crawled down his throat. Then it was gone, the dissolution almost instantaneous. He could feel nothing in his mouth as his tongue gingerly worked its way around, hoping not to encounter some undissolved fragment of that foul taste. No, that was it. In his bewildered state he wondered whether that time had come where Lardner began to rip him off, passing him dull drugs until he was forced to go through the hell of finding another supply. Or paying Lardner more money.

When he stood up to get a drink, he realised that this was not the case at all.

It began with a kind of tunnel vision. Darkness encroached from the edges of the room. Not normal darkness like the coming of night, but a deep, negative space that consumed the corners of his eyes. He sat down again quickly. His body felt normal so far but his mind raced, terrifying him with the prospect of blindness. All the awful possibilities occurred in a short space of time. Paranoid and shaking, he weathered the storm. When his body began to go limp, he lay down on the sticky remains of the couch. This is very fast, he thought. That simple idea managed to distract him from the fear of losing his sight. The growth of the dark continued inexorably. Soon he found himself staring through a pinhole into the ruins of his kitchen, out of a window, into the midday sun. Then even that was gone.

He had never experienced anything quite like this before. It still felt like an hallucination, he decided. He knew he was not truly blind. He was just in a dark place, a place without light. Except for the stars.

Ahead of him, tiny spots of light appeared. The harder he looked, the more of them he could see. Despite this, they made very little impact on the vast black expanse. Space, whether intergalactic or merely interstellar, surrounded him. A sudden sickening sensation of falling drew his attention forward, where he could see an even darker space than the ether around him. A planet loomed. He began to feel such a piercing cold in the bones he could not see that all the fears of sickness and decay came back to him. Yet it seemed impossible that anything could rot out here. Nothing could even live.

His invisible body swooped low over the planet. The grey-black ashen surface came into focus and, as his perspective improved, he saw fantastic sights. The planet was a city. Huge terraced towers ran up and down like mountain ranges, giving no impression of a level surface. Despite having no windows, Grof knew instinctively that they could only be habitations. Holes dotted the terraces. Sometimes he saw movement, but not before he was swept down the immense gullies like some plunging bird of prey. Eventually, when the stars behind him had become little more than a strip of vastly distant diamonds, he saw a river of deeper blackness running between the impossible buildings.

Then revelations came, as he plunged towards the thickening liquid, unfrozen by age or cold. Creatures flew alongside, observing him. He could feel the beat of their pale wings; hear a buzzing inside his head that he knew was a terrible communication, one he would never comprehend. Finally, as the stars disappeared behind him, he realised that one of them was his own lost midday sun.

"I want some more."

"Good. I can get it. I'm very near, in fact. I'll bring someone, the Doctor who gave the stuff to me. You'd like to meet him. Don't go anywhere."

Grof dropped the payphone without hanging it up. He stumbled up the stairs back to his rooms. His head pounded with the worst headache he could remember. His peripheral vision was still clouded with the dark but he had to have some more of the grey fungus. He was so distracted by his experience that he did not think it unusual when Lardner knocked on his door less than five minutes after his call. He was not surprised by the appearance of the Doctor either. It was as if they had been waiting.

Grof barely managed to let them in. Lardner caught him as he fell.

"Where have you been? What was it like?" asked the distinguished man who followed Lardner into the front room. Grof found himself sitting in a kitchen chair. Lardner was busying himself with something, floating around in the dark, peripheral space. The Doctor stood before him, questioning. A greying, handsome man of around sixty, he wore a brown overcoat and carried a traditional leather case. Grof felt he looked like a proper doctor, the right man to deal in fantastic drugs.

"The black planet, you've been there. It has found you."

"I want some more." Grof repeated lamely, not able to listen.

"Good, we shall go out and get you some. You only need to tell us the way. Relax. We will guide you."

Lardner finally sat down opposite the Doctor. They formed a triangle in Grof's unpleasant room. Lardner and the Doctor exchanged glances. One of them put something on the small table between them. Grof could not see what it was. There was a click. For a split second, Grof realised that it was far from over. Then the three men left on their journey.

Outside was an ancient city. It was dusk as they walked the broken cobbles of a steep, narrow street. Beyond the crumbling wall beside them, green domes and black towers slowly lit up as night came on. Grof led the way, as if he knew where to go, while Lardner and the Doctor walked behind him. None of them spoke. Grof felt, rather than heard, their suggestions on which turning to take. The headache was turning into something unmanageable. He tried not to think about it. They continued beneath towering churches, skirted overgrown orchards where small, unripe fruits fell soundlessly onto grass as they passed by. Pinnacled domes on pale buildings were behind them and before them.

When they began a steep climb, Grof looked up to see a wall of windows above him. A complex of buildings topped the headland and behind these, two of the black towers slowly disappeared as they mounted a flight of steps. They were not the hideous terraces of his previous vision but more like the spires of a cathedral, hemmed in by vast offices. Behind them, the city opened onto a sea of darkening red roofs, broken up by darker parks. Far below, at the bottom of the valley, a more normal river than the last one he had seen, complete with stone bridges and quiet, human traffic, flowed.

They wound their way up the hillside, mounting steps where necessary and negotiating sharp bends until they lost sight of all that was above them. Finally the Doctor indicated an alleyway partially covered over by scaffolding. Once they had passed underneath this, more cobbles led them to an imposing wooden door, flanked by brass plates. On closer inspection, the plates said nothing at all.

Grof looked around at his two companions. It was now almost completely night and no lights could be seen in the building before them. It twisted up and back, becoming one with all the other houses on the slope. The Doctor indicated that he should knock. Lardner smiled encouragingly. Grof took the shining metal in his hand and let it fall. There was no sound. Behind him, the doctor told Lardner that they were in Prague.

The pain in Grof's head increased dramatically when the door was opened. Lardner grasped his wrists and held him upright in an awkward position. He could hear buzzing, faint and far away.

"Where is it? Is it here?" said one of the three to whoever had opened the door. No one replied.

Once inside, a long hall stretched away to another set of double doors at the far end. To the left, an ornate spiral staircase allowed a view of the night sky through a tall window, where only the hillside should be. Lardner held Grof even tighter. The pain and the buzzing were leading him down the hall to the other doors. Before the group had stumbled more than three steps, a figure in a wheelchair emerged from under the stairs. He seemed old and pale in the inadequate light and his expression was such that it was evident he was not expecting or pleased to encounter them. He blocked their way.

"You are here then?" he enquired, looking the strange group over with an intense glare.

"The grey fungus. Do you have it here?" Grof pleaded. Lardner still held him, though he turned his head away from such pathetic pleading. The man in the wheelchair laughed out loud.

"Here? Well, perhaps, perhaps not. Follow me, I feel I must tell you something of it first." He set off toward the other doors. The unstable pair of Lardner and Grof followed, while the Doctor brought up the rear.

"Does your head hurt, young man? I would expect it does, but I doubt they told you about that, did they? You, sir, you look considerably stronger than this pitiful specimen, would you be so kind as to open the doors?".

Lardner looked back at the Doctor.

"Don't let go of him Lardner. I'll do it."

"I felt you might, good physician that you are." The man in the wheelchair smiled unpleasantly as the Doctor pushed past him to grasp the handles.

The final room -Grof felt sure he would going no further- had been painted white but was lit by only a few candles in a huge candelabra, hanging from the ceiling. The terracotta tiles of the floor showed ancient, unintelligible chalk marks of obscure occult use. A wall was given over to five great oak bookcases. A desk strewn with papers faced the one tall window that showed the city skyline in all its towered glory. The centrepiece of the room however, was a simple but immense wooden box. It stood on a crumbling altar of pink and white marble in the centre of the room and seemed to focus all the half-erased chalk marks on the floor. Grof almost cried out when he saw it. He knew the pain would stop soon. He could barely hear the old man over the buzzing noises. With alarming swiftness, the wheelchair was in front of them again.

"In 1587, Rudolf II wanted to make the lakes of Stromovka more impressive. Being a monarch of grand design, in more ways than one, he began construction of a tunnel that would lead from the Vltava River straight through the hillside to feed his precious lakes. A feat of considerable engineering, I think you'll agree. Without entering into a long description of the technicalities, I would like to paraphrase from a pamphlet written some years later by a young man in the Golden Lane under the castle, an apprentice to one of the many alchemists that lived and worked there. It is called *'Beasts Beyond Tolerance or Understanding'* and tells, with debatable clarity, a story told by the tunnelers, later corroborated and further elaborated upon by some of his master's associates.

During the second month of tunnelling, the workers found a shaft deep inside the hill. They would never have happened upon it had they not been taking the tunnel on a slight detour to avoid some particularly intransigent rock. This shaft, or fissure, was inside that rock itself. It led upward into darkness and downward into darkness. They had no idea how to proceed. The new tunnel was unconscionably rounded, bearing too much resemblance to an engineering skill well beyond their petty pick marks. They panicked and attempted to return, but in the confined space nothing was easy. The tunnel so far was no wider than three or four feet while the illumination and shoring work left much to be desired. Then the buzzing began, and the terrible smell that rose from the pit in front of them caused the first and nearest to faint, falling forward over the lip to his presumed death. There was no cry but the buzzing increased in volume. From here on the pamphlet admits to being, at best, mere hearsay, stories told over too much beer. It is said that the next man, a remarkably brave soul, obviously with no sense of smell, looked down after his fallen colleague. What he saw, rising up on membranous wings, caused him to scream, setting up insupportable echoes in the half-finished darkness. Three men lost their lives in the scramble back to the light, trampled underfoot by their friends and drowning in the inches of water on the uneven stone floor.

This is as much as could be gleaned from the sharp end, as it were. The rest our apprentice wrote down secretly and contains what he learnt from the sorcerers and alchemists that he communed with in his everyday life.

Those terrified few that found their way back to the outside world discovered, incredibly for them, that Rudolf himself was waiting. Guards, and an elite of those infamous alchemists too, were ready for them at the exit, to threaten or bribe them all into secrecy. Then, eventually, after much undisclosed preparation, these newcomers, to a man, entered the tunnel.

Later, as it was described to our young author, a shrouded, moving object was removed, crated and shipped in secret back to the Hradcany Palace. The impossible fissure was blocked and forgotten by whatever means necessary. The tunnel was continued with only a minor alteration in direction. After that, and our fellow's literary indiscretion, the legend was effectively silenced in the way only a great monarch can know. The young author merely speculates, at no great length, on Rudolf's true motives for his tunnel.

Which brings us, with a minor gap of some four hundred years, up to date, does it not? The thing in the crate, the Intolerable Beast, is not the only one of its kind; a fact, Doctor, of which you are fully aware. How else could you have started these investigations? Or indeed tracked me down in this peculiar way. It has certainly not been in my possession for the entirety of its incarceration, despite my long life. It is a fungal life form, not even entirely of this present universe, as old books would have it...but I am wasting time. Indeed, I have said more than enough, more than I would have wished, I imagine. And your friend here is all but finished. Let him loose and I shall uncover the creature. We shall witness, in a sense, a meeting of minds."

The old man reached up to the iron catches on the crate. Hoary metal creaked as the side crashed down. Grof broke free of Lardner's hold and, not believing he could still stand, stumbled toward the thing in the box.

There was glass between them even then; an extra layer of protection had been added sometime in that last four hundred years but it was clear enough, even with age and thickness. Nothing could conceal the alien nature of the beast within. It stirred, floating, as Grof held out his hand. The buzzing in his head began to resolve itself into sounds he could begin to comprehend. When he finally fell against the cool glass, the pain in his head, unbearable for so long, went out like a light. A pink and grey body slid around in the ancient prison to raise one of its many articulated limbs and scratch feebly at the place where the human hand touched the glass. A shape, a grotesquely soft conjunction of a wasp and a crab, came into view for the shortest time. Grof closed his eyes just as he saw the grey fungus growing between the folds of what passed for the Beast's head. This was what he needed. His own exhausted body fell against the Bohemian glass, while in his mind, he and the creature flying beside him dove into the black liquids of its home planet, out on the rim of the solar system.

"Is he dead?" Lardner asked.

The doctor reached under the ropes that bound Grof to the kitchen chair, feeling in vain for a pulse.

"Yes."

Lardner rose to his feet and stretched. Grof's rooms stank. It was already night outside. For seven hours he and the Doctor had been guiding the increasingly demented Grof on his visionary journey. It was tiring work. The Doctor did most of the talking, though Lardner's wrist ached from the notes he had to take. It seemed pointless, as there was a tape recorder on the table with a stack of cassettes, which they had also used. The tapes were full of Grof's whispered, elaborate descriptions, broken up by painful groans. The Doctor's voice, when it cut in with a specific question or hint, was loud and shocking. Lardner walked around the dirty room that now stank of fresh sweat as well as older, more ingrained smells. He would be glad to leave town after this.

"Was he in Prague, like you said?"

"I believe so. It appears that is where the creature is being held. It told him a good deal more than the last one we had. The tunnels, Rudolf, the timing; it all fits in with our other researches. It was clever of the Beast to make old Orne tell its story. I cannot imagine he will be appreciating the irony. It remains subtle and powerful, even now. More importantly, I am convinced that it wants me to find it."

"What about the old man? He keeps turning up."

"The Beast's current owner. Unfortunately, as a man of some occult means, he is sure to know we are coming for him. It will be extraordinarily difficult to remove the crate to another locale, though we may have to move faster than anticipated."

"Do you know who he is then?"

"In Prague? He may be Josef Nadeh, formerly Simon or Jedediah Orne. But it could all have been a disguise, his wheelchair, the alley and so on. He could do that, as he knows we are coming. He would confuse both the vision and the communion itself, if he can. He could include much that would throw us off the track, within limits. His experiments with the creature are obvious. No, we will have to travel to Prague and try again. Proximity will bring better results. I need the creature alive. What little of the fungus we get back from these investigations is not nearly enough."

"We'd better get on with it then," finished Lardner.

The Doctor reached into his case and drew out the bone saw. The top of Grof's skull needed to be removed before they could harvest the fresh growths.

The Devil's Drum

Roger Morris

A band of musicians came to town. They played strange instruments and sang in a key that no one had heard before. One day the tailor was in the crowd that came to hear.

He was a humble man who had never thought of music before. He had a wife and a little baby girl and an aged mother to look after. He spent every hour that God sent working, to put food on the table for his family.

It was not like the tailor to idle away the day. But the disturbing cadences had come in through his open window to prevent him from working.

The rhythm drew him to the front of the crowd, where he stood transfixed, unable to take his eyes off the drummer. This drummer was the tallest man the tailor had ever seen. He was dressed in splendid clothes, the colours of which flashed in time with the music. He had fierce eyes and a disquieting smile, that suggested he knew all the secrets of your heart, indeed that he knew more about you than you did yourself.

It seemed that the drummer saw the tailor too. For he beat on the skin of his drum to a tempo that matched the pace of the tailor's heart exactly.

"What I wouldn't give to play the drum like that!" said the tailor to himself.

The moment he said it the music stopped. The crowd vanished and all the other musicians too. The only two beings left on earth were the tailor and the drummer.

The drummer beat out a slow, deathly beat, that sounded like the tolling of a broken bell. He came steadily towards the tailor, though his legs did not seem to move, or at least not in the normal way.

"Would you give your aged mother?" was all that the drummer said.

"Yes," said the tailor, without a moment's hesitation. "She's old, you see, and sick and hasn't long to live. Death for her would be a kindness."

The drummer's smile changed subtly as he handed the drum to the tailor.

Then the crowd was back and all the other musicians, and the tailor was beating furiously on the skin of the drum. He had never felt such power and freedom before. He had never been alive before.

The drummer was now playing the fiddle. He winked at the tailor and smiled.

The tailor played with the musicians all day long. He forgot about his workshop and the clothes he had promised to make. Night came on, and the tailor still played. He forgot his family who sat at home and waited for him.

At last, as dawn broke, he fell down exhausted, unable to beat the drum any more.

The next thing he knew, he was being shaken into waking. He opened his eyes and saw his wife.

The musicians were gone but he still had the drum, which he started to beat as soon as he came round.

"What's got into you?" said his wife.

"Music!"

"Why didn't you come home?"

"Music!"

"Why weren't you at your workshop?"

"Music!"

"What are you doing here?"

"Music!"

And all the time he kept up a complex rhythm on the drum.

"Stop that!" She snatched the drum away from him. "Something terrible's happened."

Before she could say what it was, she burst into tears.

The tailor felt ice enter his heart. He knew what it was that had happened.

He put out a hand to comfort his wife. "Don't worry. She was old and sick and hadn't long to live. Death for her is a kindness."

"How did you know?" said his wife.

The tailor's only answer was a strange smile. He wished the ice would go away from his heart but he saw that it wouldn't. So he took back the drum and beat on it louder than ever.

"Will you come back home?" said the tailor's wife.

The tailor said that he would.

They buried his mother the following day. The day after that the tailor was back in his workshop.

He took the drum with him, intending to throw it away. But as he plied his needle, he found himself casting longing looks at the drum, which sat on his bench in front of him. And he fancied he could hear a fiddle playing a dazzling reel somewhere in the distance.

The tailor put down his needle and the suit of clothes he was working on, and took up the drum. He opened the window to hear the music more clearly. It was much closer than he had thought. Even so, it was not close enough. He climbed up on his window sill, to enter the music completely.

He had never heard anything like it.

"What I wouldn't give to play the fiddle like that!" he said to himself, for he thought the drum a sorry instrument now.

No sooner had he said it than the fiddle-player appeared beneath his window. It was the same musician who three days ago had been playing the drum. His eyes were just as fierce and his smile every bit as knowing.

"Would you give your little baby daughter?" was all that the drummer-turned-fiddle-player said.

The tailor thought for a moment. "If I knew that she was going to a better place, into the care of one who can offer her all the things I can't," reasoned the tailor with himself. "In that case it would be the right thing to do. And besides, if we find that we miss her, we can always make another child." And so the tailor said that he would.

The fiddle-player reached up a hand and lifted the tailor down. And though the tailor was not a big man, still it seemed that he had no weight at all, for the fiddle-player held him in the air as easily as a cotton bobbin.

As soon as the tailor's feet were back on the ground, the fiddle-player handed him the fiddle. To his amazement, the tailor found he knew just where to put his fingers and just how to hold the bow. When he started to play, a note came out of the instrument that was as pure and strong as any that the fiddle-player had produced. Within minutes the tailor was playing the dazzling reel. The fiddle-player winked and smiled and tapped his foot. Then he started to sing, and his voice was surprisingly high and beautiful, the most affecting falsetto that you have ever heard.

The tailor walked the streets of the town playing reel after reel on the fiddle. All the time, the fiddle-player-turned-singer walked by his side, singing as he went.

A crowd of malevolent-faced children followed them. Once or twice, the tailor thought he saw his baby daughter being passed between them. But he didn't know how that could be and these children had such malevolent faces that he preferred not to look at them. The tailor wondered where the children came from, for he had never seen them in the town before. As if to answer his thoughts, the singer broke off from his singing and cried gleefully: "They're mine!"

The tailor walked the streets all night and once again fell down exhausted, just as dawn was breaking.

When he woke a few hours later the fiddle was still in his hands. Indeed, the strings of the fiddle were still hot from the scorching tunes he had played. The singer and his children were gone.

The tailor ran his fingers up and down the neck of the fiddle. He was amazed to find that he could still play the instrument. Only one thing spoilt his pleasure: the image of his baby daughter being passed between the singer's children.

He was afraid to go back home but knew that he must.

They buried the little baby girl the following day. A month after that the tailor was back in his workshop.

He took the fiddle with him, though he had not touched it for a month.

It was cold in the workshop, colder than he ever remembered it.

Three times he held the needle to the light. Three times he held the thread to the needle. But he could not darn it. His fingers trembled so much from the cold.

"What I need is a fire," said the tailor to himself. He looked around for something to burn.

His glance fell upon the fiddle. Intending to smash it for tinder, he picked the instrument up. But as soon as his fingers touched the wood, they ceased to tremble. He was no longer cold. A fire had entered him.

As he played, he heard the striking falsetto. It was strangely muted, as distant as the hills, and as close as his own breath, like the voice we have all heard in our childhood, calling our name when we are alone in an empty place.

The tailor stopped playing and listened. The singing continued. It soothed away all his unhappiness.

"What I wouldn't give to be able to sing like that!" said the tailor to himself.

No sooner had he spoken than the singing stopped. Instead he could hear something thrashing away inside the chimney breast.

This sound gave way to silence. Then suddenly the drummer-turned-fiddle-player-turned-singer's head appeared upside down in the fireplace.

"Would you give your wife?"

"What kind of a monster do you think I am?" cried the tailor. "My wife, my mate, my one true love. When I think of her sitting at home. Eating herself up with grief, she is. Yes, in all honesty, she has not been herself since you took the baby. There's nothing I can do to make it up to her. What can I do? I can't bring back the child, can I? I'd burn this fiddle in an instant if I thought it would do any good. But it won't. I know that. No. The kindest thing I could do would be to let you take her so that she can be with the baby and look after it. That's what she'd want, I'm sure. It would be a terrible loss for me to bear, naturally. But if I had the singing, if I could sing like that... "

The singer's eyes grew as bright as burning coals. Then there was a fire in the grate and he was gone.

The tailor called out, "Hello?" The word came out in a singing tone, an major scale ascending on the "Hell-", a minor scale descending on the "-lo".

The tailor did not go home that night. He did not go home ever again. He left his workshop and wandered the land, a minstrel. From that first tentative performance, he soon progressed to a repertoire of popular songs of the day.

His fame spread far and wide. He never knew want or hunger again. But he was not satisfied, though he drank to excess and ate to excess and had many women. He realised that he envied the very songs he sang. He could sing the musical notes but he could not become them. And there was in them an honesty and a purity that he wanted.

One night he leapt from a strange bed in a strange inn and threw open the windows and shouted at the top of his voice: "What I wouldn't give to become the music!"

He had not seen the drummer-turned-fiddle-player-turned-singer for some years. In fact, he had begun to doubt his existence. It was possible to explain everything that had happened without the intervention of the other.

As he was thinking this, he noticed two bright stars burning at opposite ends of the sky. As he watched, the two stars moved slowly towards each other. The tailor now saw that they were not stars, but the glowing eyes of the drummer-turned-fiddle-player-turned-singer, whose face had appeared, along with the rest of him, suspended in mid air just outside the window. As usual, the disquieting smile was in place.

"Let me see if I understand you," said the floating figure. "You say you wish to become the music. By that, you mean - what exactly? A haunting melody hanging in the air? A trumpet blast? The shrill warble of a marching fife? What signature, what measure, what tempo? Have you given any thought to these things?"

"I wish to be music. To exist as music. All music. Everywhere."

"I have never... in all my years as the evil one - of course, you knew all along who I was, didn't you?... this really does take the biscuit..."

"Is it possible?"

"Anything's possible. Provided you are prepared to pay the price."

"What price?"

"Your soul."

"What use do you have for souls?"

"I feed on them. I chew them and suck them. And swallow them and digest them. And defecate them."

"But my soul will be in the music."

"Then I must have the music. All music. Everywhere. It must become mine."

The tailor thought for a moment. If the devil had all music, there would be none left for anyone else.

"How about if I just become the tunes. Just the good ones, say."

The devil's face brightened. "The best ones?"

The tailor nodded.

"Come now. I am hungry," said the devil. His strange smile spread across the sky. And his teeth sparkled like sharp little stars.

Urban Sabbatical

Michael Laimo

While waiting for his wife to return from a tour of the city, Corbin sipped a gin and tonic on the balcony of the hotel suite. He'd been encouraged to accompany Roberta and her associate Darren Heller on the two-hour excursion, but decided to pass on the opportunity. Darren's wife Camille was inside fixing dinner for the four of them.

For an hour Corbin had been staring out over the lights of Manhattan. He hadn't wanted to visit New York in the first place, with or without the Hellers. Nothing against them. He simply detested the concrete jungle, especially in this section where he'd been invited to stay for the past two weeks. Just apartments and skyscrapers. No trees. No plants. No animals. Just a gray, dismal landscape.

And August in New York was simmering hot. Damn it, he felt like a heel for allowing Roberta to convince him to leave Myrtle Beach. You only get one summer off a year, he argued, and despite the fact the opportunity meant the world to his wife, he'd give the sweaty shirt off his back right now to be vacationing with her somewhere along the coast of lake Ontario instead.

People leave the city to vacation, not go to it.

Heat and exhaust rose from the street in visible layers, the cars and trucks laboring through as if gasping with distress. It sifted high through the air so even the statues and buildings appeared to choke, the pigeons roosting on the eaves bowing their heads in torment, pleading for compassion.

Through the city's muggy breaths came a knock on the balcony door.

When Corbin turned he saw a black man standing just beyond glass partition. Corbin had seen a great deal of strangely exotic people during his two-week stay in New York, but had paid them no genuine interest. Here in the vicinity of his temporary and somewhat sterile haven, the man's presence was a bit jarring. He stood at least six-three, and entered the balcony on thickly calloused bare feet. In his arms he carried a motionless Chihuahua.

Quite a laughable twosome, Corbin thought. Though he resented his wife for dragging him into this gargantuan mess-alopolis, he induced a welcoming smile.

The black man made their encounter non-welcoming, pressing his face against the dog's muzzle and whispering utterances in Creole.

Corbin had learned a few words of the Haitian language by default, living with a woman whose obsession with the culture ran to all extremes. Roberta had admonished him for not sharing her enthusiasm for the world's 'most intriguing civilization', insisting that he, at the very least, show *some* interest in her passion. *I'm a schoolteacher for Christ's sake,* he'd argue. *And if I were an anthropologist, I'd delve into more pleasurable areas, like Hawaii or Cabo.* She'd shrug off his indifference to general pigheadedness and march off upstairs to read up on Haitian customs and language.

Here, all he could do was mimic the Chihuahua's somber expression and wait until the whispering verbiage ceased. He peered into the suite and called for some support.

"Camille! I believe our guest has arrived! Would you please come out here before I laugh in his face?" He gazed at the man and added, "If you'd have come a week ago, I'd be home by now."

Camille Heller stepped out onto the balcony wearing a sauce-spotted apron, holding a ladle. She was attractive, slim with dark brown hair, bubbling with vigor at the very appearance of their visitor. Roberta, Camille, and Darren had ventured together on two other funded sabbaticals in the past, one to South Africa and the other to Venezuela. When Camille called and revealed that Harvard had subsidized a trip to New York, Corbin questioned the validity of such a furlough.

It's for a project we've been working on, Roberta explained. *And this time I'd like for you to come.*

Gazing at the strange black man and his dog, he questioned it even more.

Camille held a very lively discussion with the stranger in Creole, then turned towards Corbin, her face ablaze with excitement. "It's official!"

"What's official?"

"We've been invited to a Haitian voodoo ceremony, right here in Manhattan!"

"Oh, good God. Are you kidding me? Isn't that taking things a bit too far?"

"And I would like for you to come." Roberta's voice filtered in from behind the stranger. Peering around the Haitian's body, Corbin saw his wife glaring at him, Darren Heller at her shoulder.

"No Roberta. Uh-uh," he said, pointing his gin and tonic. "You never told me about...about this!"

"You would have never come to New York if I did."

"Well I'm not going anywhere, especially with this *freak*."

"Well I'm attending. Whether you decide to go is your business." She tramped back into the suite. A frowning Camille followed, leaving Corbin alone with the Haitian and his tiny dog.

Corbin smiled weakly. The black man ignored him, whispering secrets to his dog.

There was much to consider. If he stayed behind then he would have to entertain himself for the night until the three of them returned from the so-called ceremony. He'd have to prepare his own meal, or eat out alone without a soul to talk to. And then the city with the heat and the awful smells and all the hustle and bustle—it would just about send him over the edge. And besides all that, having to deal with an angry Roberta would not be a pleasurable way to end the trip. She'd hold it against him for weeks.

The next evening, following a hearty meal and considerable supply of mixed drinks, the four of them left by cab with the Chihuahua-toting envoy relaying directions. He went by the name Namor, and he spent the last eighteen hours on his knees in prayer in one of the suite's three bedrooms. The ride took them to the outskirts of the city, past Harlem and well into the heart of the Bronx. Once there Namor guided them into a subway station where they made three stops. Corbin was nervous in the squalid environment, but Darren and Camille's sociological work in New England's worse areas had the two of them taking the journey in stride. Roberta's wandering eyes told him that she was savoring the cultural experience.

Contemptfully, Corbin took in the hot, horrid stenches of New York's underground, the variety of colorful people and the potential threat they carried with them, all the while trying to share in his wife's enthusiasm, to imagine what everyone else might be thinking and how they could possibly be enjoying the experience. He failed to find any satisfaction in the moment, seeing only the inside of a stained subway car as it ground to a stop at their destination.

Namor led them out into a gray deserted street; a neighborhood lined with abandoned tenements and stripped vehicles. They made a quickened approach towards the entrance of one building with its brick facing lost beneath layering of colorful graffiti. The windows were long shattered, leaving iron bars as the only means for security.

In the entranceway rats and insects roamed freely like house pets, some of them, Corbin imagined, ending up as meals for the local children. Trash filled the place, age-old phone books swollen and stained, crushed cans, shattered bottles littering the floor. Corbin considered retrieving a shard of glass for a weapon, just in case, but had no time as Namor quickly ushered them into a stairwell.

The odor here was hot and foul, assaulting Corbin's gorge as he fought back a bitter mix of bile and gin. The group remained quiet as their footsteps echoed their ascension of four flights, and when the stairs went no further they came into a hallway. "We are here," Namor informed them, then entered into the first room on the left.

This undoubtedly was the voodoo locale. The walls to the two adjacent apartments had been torn down, creating one very large area. The floor had been completely blanketed in hard-packed soil, twigs, leaves, rotting flowers and fruits littering it in scattered heaps. Mosquitoes buzzed about the place in clouds, seeking to mount themselves upon the new, fresh-smelling visitors.

A black man about the same size and height of Corbin approached from behind a brown curtain draped at the bathroom entrance, scowling and grunting in foreign tongue. Corbin backed away, gripping Roberta's arm, repulsed at the shocking sight of him. "Namor, what's he gibbering about?"

"He is the man of mission. The houngan. He says he can make the insects go away, if you prefer."

Corbin swatted at the mosquitoes, now making a meal of his arms. "Tell him I said yes. I prefer if he makes them go away." The houngan was disfigured to an extent Corbin could have never imagined in even his wildest nightmares. Glistening in sweat, his face looked as if it had been severely burned, long flaps of skin dangling from his cheeks and brow like strips of uncooked bacon. His nose was horribly misshapen, full and potato-like with pinholes for nostrils. And then his eyes, one orb gazing out from where his left eyebrow should have been, the other lower, in the cheek area. Only when Corbin managed to tear his sights away from his face did he realize that the man wore little more than a loincloth to hide his privates.

Corbin nearly pulled Roberta out of the room but the houngan howled like a wolf and waved his arms about in an odd tribal dance. The intimidating ritual lasted fifteen seconds, freezing Corbin, and then he backed away.

"Are you ready?" Namor asked the four of them. All but Corbin nodded. He burped gin again and noticed a crowd of robe-clad people gathering by a table set up at the opposite end of the room. Namor led the four of them to the center of the room, Corbin taking a moment to brush a few dead mosquitoes from his shirt.

Two perspiring men draped in white covered the table with a black tablecloth. They arranged eight candles in a circular pattern, lit them, and then placed a bottle filled with liquid and four glasses in the center. Namor pulled Camille Heller aside for a brief discussion in Creole, then disappeared into the growing crowd of perhaps twenty people.

"What's going on?" Corbin asked Roberta. "I'm hot and queasy and I want to leave."

Camille leaned over. "There's a bit of a problem."

"Does this mean we can leave?"

Roberta nudged her husband. "Behave," she whispered.

"The ritual is about to begin," Camille revealed. "Namor said the houngan is not all that comfortable with our presence. He feels we might be a risk to his service."

"Great," Corbin muttered.

"Then we really must be on our best behavior," Roberta added, eying her husband.

"Didn't he know we were coming?" Darren asked.

"Yes, but he is still ill-at-ease. Namor couldn't be specific as to why."

Corbin leaned forward and said in a low voice, "So let's just leave then."

All three of them shook their heads. "We can't," Roberta said. "It would be a great insult to withdraw our invitation at this stage, and the houngan would take great offense regardless of how he feels about our presence. This service has been arranged exclusively for us. Just be careful what you say or do, and everything will be fine."

"We really wouldn't want to insult him," Darren added. There was a tremor of discomfort in his voice.

A strange odor filled the room. A shuffling ensued and Corbin saw four men carrying in a huge vat of steaming liquid.

"What's that?"

"Oil," Darren said. "It is boiled to help summon..." He turned towards his wife. "Camille, I wasn't expecting this—"

"I wasn't either."

Corbin wore an uncomfortable grin. "What? What is it?"

Camille looked concerned. "This is more than just a voodoo ceremony. By the looks of it I'd say we're about to witness a black magic ritual. The Devil's toil."

Camille added, "Which also means that man is not just a houngan. He's a high-priest."

"Oh, you can't be serious," Corbin said. His stomach turned and the gin came up in his throat, forming a hot acidic ball. He swiped the sweat from his forehead. He didn't like this one bit.

Camille leaned in close to everybody. "Listen, these people take this initiation quite seriously. I might add that what we're about to see could be quite shocking, so please, just sit back and do what they say. Understand?"

"Understood," Corbin said, quite apprehensively.

Night had fallen. The only light in the room came from the candles burning on the table. The mosquitoes returned, buzzing in frenzy as if in anticipation of the event. A large block of wood about four feet high painted in many glossy colors had been centered next to the table, as if placed to discourage anyone from taking that spot.

"That's where the sacrifice will take place," Camille revealed. "It unites the mortals with the dead."

"Sacrifice! What is this? Roberta, please, let's leave!"

"Corbin!" Roberta muttered in panic. "Don't move. Don't do anything."

"Damn it! I'm *very* uncomfortable."

"I am too, but remember, we are guests. As long as we keep our mouths shut, all will be fine."

Corbin blew out a nervous breath. "I didn't know your enthusiasm ran to this extreme."

A few more people dressed in black entered the room and then the doors were shut. The high-priest appeared again from behind the brown curtain and retrieved the bottle from the table. Pouring out the syrupy contents, he drew a rough circle in the soil on the ground before the wood block. One of the participants lit a fire atop the surface of the vat of oil. The cobalt flame painted the walls in a ghostly phosphorescent glow. The room immediately smelled of burning oil.

The high-priest began an exotic song of prayer, pouring the liquid from the bottle into the four glasses on the table. Filling them halfway, he completed this stage of the initiation by quickly shaking his hands in the air.

"This phase provides us with sect acceptance," Camille explained quietly. "Without this we wouldn't be permitted to participate."

When the high-priest retreated from the table, two black-clad men brought the glasses over to the four of them. "Drink it," Camille said, taking a glass.

The men before them nodded. Corbin looked at the brown liquid. "Here goes nothing." He swilled it in one shot. Thick. Sweet-tasting spirits. A mix between rum and amaretto. He handed the glass back to the man in black, taking in a deep breath as the alcohol seeped to his stomach. He looked at Roberta, grinned. "Not bad."

The high-priest ran his hands across his face. A man dressed in a red robe separated from the crowd and stood before the master of ceremonies, eyes turned upward, the whites exposed. Drums sounded from an unseen area and then the prayer began, the entire crowd chanting in unison. It went on like this for perhaps five minutes before the drums slowly tapered, then ceased altogether. The crowd remained still. Soon dead silence filled the room.

The man in red removed his robe, exposing his nakedness.

In the meantime Corbin had caught quite a buzz. The drink the high-priest had given him wasn't cooperating with the gin in his stomach. Closing his eyes, he forced back a gag. When he opened his eyes, the naked man was kneeling before the colorful block in a solemn, prayerful position, tongue stuck out and pressed against the flat wood surface. The high-priest leaned before him, a hand-held razor in his grasp. In one sudden flick of the wrist, he thrust the razor down and split the man's tongue down the center, forking it. Blood sputtered in a geyser, darkening the block. The drums resumed, along with the chanting.

The initiate staggered up and backed away from the high-priest, blood pouring down his chin. As the chanting culminated to an emphatic point, he slowly walked over to the vat of fiery oil. He climbed in, feet first, fully immersing himself in seconds.

Steam spurted up from the vat: a shocking spout, rife with the stench of burning flesh.

The nightmarish scene propelled Corbin to the climax of his nausea. Dizzied and stunned, he reeled forward and collided with the high-priest, sending the man to the soil-packed floor. A forbidding silence seized the room. Corbin was too sick to notice. Hunched over and blinded by the smoke, he vomited on the squirming voodoo-master.

Trembling, Corbin peered up, saliva on his chin. His eyes were filled with stinging tears. Darkened faces stared at him, flickering candlelight dancing across them. *Fear* consumed the room, and the thick stink of cooked man was making him sick again.

The high-priest scrambled up, pushing his vomit-slathered chest out as if showing Corbin the evidence of the travesty he just committed. He was seething, hot breaths spouting from his twisted mouth like dragon's snorts. Yelling in Creole, he confronted Corbin, arms flailing. Corbin tried to yell his defense, but it did him no avail. Squealing like pig, the high-priest abruptly lunged forward.

Corbin defended himself quickly, greeting the assault with two quick fists, one to the collarbone, the other to the side of the head. The voodoo-master collapsed to the floor in a crumpled heap, writhing in agony, cursing in tongues. Corbin lunged away from the altar across the room, looking back to see if Roberta and the Hellers were following. Indeed they were, their faces twisted with fear and revulsion.

He also caught one last glimpse of the gnarled face of the high-priest, his lopsided eyes staring out from beneath his death-mask, steadily fixed on Corbin. Corbin shuddered, inflicted with the horrible feeling that those vindictive eyes possessed were drilling terrible poisons into him. He twisted away in terror and stumbled into the hall, down the steps and out into the heat-stricken night, where he threw up again, all over his shoes.

He came to in the suite, the soft mattress a welcome relief to his aching body. Roberta was sitting in a chair next to him, staring at him in silence. At first he recalled the displaced eyes of the houngan pinning him, warning him of something secretive as he rushed from the ceremony. Now, in his waking, he saw his wife's troubled gaze revealing to him nothing less than a dozen pent-up emotions. She got up and sat on the edge of the bed, placing a gentle hand on his forehead.

"How do you feel?"

"Lousy. Hung over. My head is killing me."

"Too much gin—"

"It was that stuff we drank last night." With great effort Corbin wriggled up and gazed about the room. A single lamp in the foyer sent a dim yellow light across the room. The curtains were open slightly, enough to see the darkness outside. "Damn, it's still night?"

"*Still* night? You slept through the day."

"What? How can that be? How long have I been asleep?"

"About twenty hours. You're sick, Corbin. You're running a high fever. You must have been coming down last night. It's probably why you threw up."

Corbin smacked his lips. "Ugh, I can still taste my puke. Can I have some water?"

Roberta nodded then left the room. Corbin closed his eyes and massaged his damp forehead, thinking about the disaster he caused at the ritual. Now he feared for everyone's safety, realizing the seriousness of his reckless act. Roberta returned with a glass of water. The Hellers were right behind her.

"How're feeling Corb?" Darren asked.

"Like shit on a stick." He took the water from Roberta. "Is everything okay?"

The three of them looked at each other, then at Corbin. "We hope so," Camille said. "I haven't heard from Namor. That worries me. No doubt he's been reprimanded for bringing us into their private circle. And to think it had taken me months of convincing him there would be nothing to worry about."

"What about ugly? I hit him pretty hard."

Why am I worried about the freak? What about the poor bastard that...

"Hey, wait a second. That guy from the ceremony, the one who climbed into the oil?"

His question received blank stares in reply.

"The guy who got his tongue split by the ugly voodoo guy?"

Roberta placed a hand on his forehead. "What are you talking about Corbin?"

He looked at the others in the room, their gazes unflinching as if her were a freak-show oddity. "The naked guy. He came in; the voodoo priest cut his tongue with a razor. Then he climbed into that big oil bath? C'mon, how can you not remember?"

"He's really burning up," Roberta said. Camille left and returned a moment later with a tray. "Here's some toast and rice, orange juice and aspirin. It will help the fever."

Corbin dropped his head back onto the pillow. Having this conversation had exhausted him, and now he felt like sleeping again. "I didn't dream it. I'm telling you..."

"We're going to get some dinner, hon. we'll be back shortly. Call me on the cell if you need anything. Okay?"

"Hmph."

Corbin fell back asleep.

Corbin awoke with the terrible taste of vomit in his mouth. In the darkness of the bedroom he could barely make out the outline of the untouched food tray on the nightstand. He fidgeted up on his elbows, the stench of puke thick in his nostrils. Had he vomited in his sleep? Dizzy. The fever had culminated. He was burning up.

Sweat trickled down his face and back. A high-pitched whining sound zipped by his right ear. *Mosquitoes. Damn, how'd the hell they get in here?* It took a great effort to swipe them away, his muscles tingling painfully, numbed. Spasms lanced through his cracking bones.

He wiped the sweat from his face. His hand came away soaked.

Something feels different...

He went back to his brow, to his cheeks and chin, prodding the skin. What began as curiosity quickly culminated into terror as his fingers surveyed the landscape of his face: the tender meaty texture of it, the twisted flaplets of skin...

Dear God, please tell me I'm hallucinating. In the dark, he stumbled out of bed down the short hall to the bathroom. Dizziness nearly sent him to the floor. He flicked the lights and peered at his face in the mirror. *Oh my God...*

His skin. It was virtually gone. In its place, bleeding blisters. Globules of pussing fluids. Strips of tattered flesh. His hair, reduced to a few singed wisps.

Dazed from fever or not, he couldn't deny the change of his appearance. Nor could he withhold the fact that the few remaining tatters of skin on his face were no longer white. He looked at his arms, his hands. They were blackened, charred.

Dear God, it looks as if I've been...burned.

No longer able to think, he staggered into the shower, peeling away his tee shirt, his shorts. His entire body was blackened and blistering. His legs, stomach, shoulders. *Everywhere.* Even his privates, shriveled away. He ran the cold water. It attacked his burning body like falling needles, steam rising as it sizzled on his skin. Unable to cool off, he stepped from the shower and re-examined his body in the mirror. The person staring back at him was wide-eyed with fear, a man who had been severely burned and lived to tell about it. This was a man who should have been dead. He tried to scream. The only thing to emerge from his mouth was a bloated black tongue.

We're about to witness a black magic ritual, Camille had said.

Again Corbin thought of the man who immersed himself in the boiling oil. Why didn't anyone else remember him? *Why?*

Fleeting snippets of the ritual besieged him:

Listen, these people take this initiation quite seriously.

The high priest is not pleased with our presence. He feels we are a danger to his service.

We must be on our best behavior then.

Drink it. It gives us sect acceptance.

Corbin reeled into the bedroom. Still naked and burning up, he flung himself onto the bed. His skin screamed. Again he tried to yell but could not, his tongue filling his mouth. He tasted vomit, then recalled, I threw up the drink of acceptance...

He heard the door of the suite open. The lively chatter of Camille, Darren, his wife, and—and—

Who is that other voice?

Weren't they worried about him? Why weren't they coming in here to check up on him? He needed help. He needed them. He smelled the sheets on the bed. They were beginning to smolder.

Corbin finally managed a weak yell, a muted blare barely making it past his swollen tongue.

Silence inside.

Footsteps. The light came on in the bedroom.

Darren Heller appeared, a look of shock and revulsion on his face. "Oh my God..."

"What is it Darren?" Roberta.

Corbin tried to speak. He couldn't. He could only twitch his fingers and toes.

Then the rest of them appeared. Camille. Then Roberta.

Then Corbin.

The man standing next to his wife was an exact replica of himself. To the tee. Just like he was to...

To the man at the ritual. The one who climbed into the oil.

Camille and Roberta fled in tears, screaming who is he? and what's happened to him? Darren ran from the room, calling for help.

Leaving Corbin alone in the room with his twin. Corbin.

The twin Corbin walked over to the bed, staring. He rubbed a gentle finger on his chin. And smiled.

Inside, Corbin heard the police arrive.

The last thing Corbin saw before the police came to take him away was his twin taunting him, licking his red lips with a long, forked tongue.

Dream Boy

Jack Fisher

The Dream Boy decided it would be his last stop of the night. He swooped down from the shadow-heavens with his brilliant lime green eyes and a syrupy mouth full of razors. He curled out from between the glowing phosphorescent stars, moons, and comets that were stuck to young Logan Matthews' bedroom ceiling like a tendril of wood smoke. He wore a cape of leaves and dandelions and wiggled his candlestick fingers. His irises glowed rainbow-tornadoes that lit up his face. He came just when Logan was dreaming—REMing—with his eyes twitching and quivering.

The Dream Boy descended quietly—his veiny dragonfly wings fluttering faster than a hummingbird's—just inches above Logan's head, breathing heavily. A dream seeped out of Logan's ear, fell, and scurried underneath the fat pillow like a roach. The Dream Boy smiled. He wiggled the stardust from his fingers, and, with the grace of the Tooth Fairy, he snatched it up. It was blue and charged electric. The Dream Boy flicked it up into the air like a quarter, opened his mouth, and down it slid. Logan woke up the next morning and on his pillow, it looked like a blue crayon had been melted and dripped over it.

Over seas in an ancient land, in the humid, melancholy mists of sorrow, the Dream Boy was hunched in a vast field of dandelions with a honeybee breeze flitting his leaf cape, flapping. He sneezed and a dozen dreams sprayed out; he coughed, gagged, and a few more flew out; he held his nose, blew, and a couple more dropped out.

They lay, buzzing and shivering on the ground, some hot pink, fluorescent, purple, blue, and some black. The black ones had been thieved from the minds of the diseased. They were crisp and charred, black and curled like raisins and they beat like little hearts. The Dream Boy stomped the black ones, ground and twisted them under his foot, growling.

Once the Dream Boy stole the dream from a little brat who stirred beehives then threw kittens near them and threw lit matches and cigarette butts at dogs. For a change, he lifted this one's eyelid and he could see what the boy was thinking, he could read his thoughts, and discern his dreams. When he saw what the boy was about to dream, he grabbed him by the hair, twisted his skull back, plastered his moldy mouth over the boy's, and sucked out any dream that was untoward or malicious.

The dream lay like a mucus-muscle, entombing the kid's brain. It peeled off as easy as the shell from a hardboiled egg and tasted like placenta. The brat woke up gasping for air just in time—the Dream Boy had taken what he had come for. He turned into a moth and bumped his way out the open, airy window.

When the Dream Boy got back to his domain, he spit up the febrile mess. Upon closer inspection, he noticed that it had taken the form of a slick, slimy fetus-skeleton with an oversized skull and black, alien eyes. He splattered it under his foot and the wild bat-dogs that roamed the vast plains would lap up the mess in a few hours. It was always the *bad* dream that gave him the distasteful side effects after ingesting them and regurgitating them: yellow bile, vomitus, and stomach upset.

Another night of collecting.

The Dream Boy took what was left of the good dreams and threaded them into elaborate dream necklaces, all shiny and sparkling (he wore a different one every night). And when he was done with his nightly routine it was especially cold and dim. He unthreaded one of the gumdrop dreams and popped it into his mouth, sat back, let it melt under his tongue, and allowed for ecstasy dreams, a dream retold through the eyes and mouth of a phantom narrator. Dreams of little boy's and girl's, of rainbows and marbles, kittens and cat, puppies and dogs, demon creatures, albino-white and shivering with fever in the dark corners of their room, stealing quick glances back at the particular sleeping babe and smiling...

With each passing trip, he would unthread another and flick it into his razor-lined mouth, each better than the next until he came to one in particular. Without looking, he dropped it in. This one seized the Dream Boy. His long, frail fingers clawed at the ground, clear fingernails snapped and bled as they rubbed into the dirt. His throat spasmed, his eyes twitched and spun malevolently, his body was rigid.

The dream melted black acid under his tongue and seeped subcutaneously into the thick, purple veins under his pink tongue.

He was in an open field under a dark, overcast sky. Gawking figures in black top hats with painted-white faces cackled and asked him to die, rats chewed off his fingers, bees crawled out of his nostrils, got caught in his nares, and stung his lips. Flowers of exquisite rot-blossoms grew from his cheeks and burst forth hundreds upon hundreds of baby spiders, flaming angels fell from the skies and landed like dead doves next to him, everyone of them still partially alive and screaming. The Dream Boy woke from his own dream, screaming. It was when someone—or something—whispered into his ear that the man in the moon had been murdered that made him break from his awful reverie.

In a land of faraway, far from his, someone was dreaming. The Dream Boy *sensed* it. He stood, shook off the dusty bad-dream remnants from his exterior, and took a deep breath. His wings, with a mind and dreams all of their own, began to tremble, then buzz, then flap. And the Dream Boy was off again to collect only delicious, warm, and glowing dreams.

Then, after every visit, he hung dream catchers in every window.

Gold Nuggets

Barbara Malenky

Cassie Mae moved slowly over the muddy ground trying in vain to avoid soiling her boots. The distance between the dance hall and the row of privies was a couple of hundred yards and it was quite treacherous a journey after a rainfall.

It wasn't a question of going. She had to do that, but had waited a little too long, and was now moving too fast to prevent mud from splashing on her.

She lifted the hem of her taffeta dancing dress between her forefingers and thumbs. There wasn't much she could do to protect her crinoline, so she cursed the mud quietly, a habit caught from her customers who worked the local mines. The string of vulgarity made her feel better. Her lantern swung along her arm and as if to retaliate, a sudden breeze blew it out.

The rain had stopped. There was a pale sinister fog draped over the tops of the shanty boxes that straddled Turtle Creek. She could hardly make them out. Hesitating, she tried counting off to what she thought would be the third one. It was her favorite, there being an actual wooden seat rounding the hole. The girls of Red Heaven House made fun of her, but

Cassie Mae had brought her love of city niceties right along with her to New Mexico when she left Kansas City six months ago. If doing her nature calls while seated on a piece of real pine was possible, then Cassie Mae would do so, and the others be damned.

There were crudely made plank walkways leading to each box and Cassie Mae located one under her boot and tread carefully up to the door. She pulled on the handle.

"Body in here," bellowed a whiskey-soaked voice.

"Oh," she whispered, and moved to the next one.

"It ain't vacant," another voice answered at her pull on the door.

She took a step back. She still wasn't sure which building held the wooden seat, but she decided to wait for it.

The fog swirled softly around her like down. It lent a beauty that she found happy to look at and she entertained herself by mentally arranging rolls of mist into objects. To her right were white satin shoes like the ones she had once seen on a lady in Kansas City. And near her left the fog swirled into a big hat with fluffy white plumes of feathers. It was the kind wealthy city women wore to Sunday church services. If she stared straight into the fog she was sure to catch sight of a silvery dress of fine velvet, the one she dreamt of someday wearing as a bride. In the fog, everything was possible.

A loud boom jerked her back into reality. A large and panting man crashed out from one of the privies. His large boots sank down into the mud as he passed her and sent a spray of it against the bottom of her dress.

"You beast," she called after him, but he disappeared inside the fog like a dead man's ghost. She came closer and peered inside the little building. No, it wouldn't do. It was a straddler; a flat plank floor with a double hole. She stepped back to wait.

Returning to her game, Cassie Mae wondered what the reaction would be if she reemerged inside the dance hall wearing the beautiful velvet wedding dress. How she would dance then. No man could resist her and she would be twirled and held tight, to later retire on the arms of the most desired gentleman in the room. A man who, while Cassie Mae remained in her room to pack, would go to the madam and insist on buying her away. It would be a new life with wealth and a man so in love he could help her become a lady.

"Guess it's all yorn," a gruff voice said as a figure came from the building, slammed shut the door and went past her. "Better hold yer nose, honey. It's mighty pawerful in thar."

Cassie Mae sighed. She pinched her nostrils together and took hold the handle. She peered through the darkness, trying to see the wooden seat.

A dark figure stepped in front of her.

"Oh," she cried. "I believe I was next." It was hard not to swing at the man for being so rude, but then, by this time of the night, the rowdy men were all drunk out of their minds. Sometimes they couldn't distinguish the difference between a man and woman.

The man took hold of Cassie Mae's arm and pulled her roughly inside the outbuilding and up against him. She didn't have time to do more than open her mouth and let out one small squeak before his lips pressed hard over hers and drowned out any other protest.

"Be quiet," he whispered when he let her lips free. "I'm not going to hurt you. I need your help, missy." His arms were strong and still held her tight. She gasped for breath, unable to speak. "I've been watching you dancing in there and you've got the attention of someone I've been looking for a long time. I can make it worth your while if you do what I say. You need to stay quiet. Understand?"

She nodded and he let her free. In the confines of the little building they were still very close together and she became aware of his musky odor that spoke of long hours in the saddle and nights in the wilderness.

"Can I light my lantern?" she asked, hopeful.

"It's best you don't see me, missy," he answered, his voice low and rough. "You won't be able to place a finger on me that way. Now listen careful, I got a bag here full of gold nuggets..." a heavy clinking sound gave his words meaning. "You can have it if you do what I say." He reached for her hand and placed the soft leather pouch between her fingers. She could feel the solid chunks rolling against each other. They were large and filled her with strange longing.

"What did he do?" she managed, intoxicated by the feel of the gold.

"Never you mind on that," the man whispered. "Think what a girl like you can do with wealth like this. You got some dreams better than what you got right now. You got an old mama somewhere or a little brother you could help out. You got your eye on a life where you don't need wear out your beauty on these old drunks. You got some dreams and all you need do is help me fulfill mine."

"What do you want me to do?" Cassie Mae asked softly, remembering the purity of the white velvet-wedding gown. "I ain't gonna be part of a killing, mister. I'm a good girl."

"And you'll stay that way. Now here's the plan..."

The musicians were playing a cross-eyed snap when Cassie Mae returned to the dance hall. She had barely crossed the floor when several hands grabbed for her and took her away in a frenzied foot race. She danced until she couldn't breathe, managing finally to pull away from the crowd and seek shelter behind the stairs. Her eyes scanned the floor. It wasn't long.

"There you are, little darling," his loud voice announced and two big hands reached behind the stairs to catch Cassie Mae under the arms and lift her out into the opening. "I'm ready for a dance with the prettiest little girl in the Red Heaven and I aim to get it." Absolam Monroe was a big man with wide shoulders and a red complexion. He had small red lips and thinning dark hair. He twirled her about and took her across the dance floor with the energy of a man younger than his forty-odd years.

When he was winded he pulled her along to the side and produced a silver flask from his coat pocket. He took a long drink then set his small dark eyes lustily on her.

"A gal like you deserves better than this, honey." He leaned in close to her. He smelled like old dirt. "I had a little talk with the proprietor of this establishment about you. She tells me you wouldn't mind making a man happy if he had the notion to make your life steady. What do you say about it?"

Cassie Mae tried to flirt, but her eyes jerked about the room in nervous anxiety. She wasn't at all sure she could carry this off. But then the feel of the nugget bag won out and she flashed her eyes at Absolam and said, "I can't think at all in this smoky room. Why don't we take a walk outside where the air is moist." She took hold of his hand for good measure and tugged him along behind her. "I'll be proud to listen to you out there."

He had arrived earlier at the Red Heaven with two other men, both rough cut characters that stood contently at the bar while Absolam pursued his pleasures. When they saw him heading along behind Cassie Mae they downed their shots of whiskey and came too.

"Oh no," Cassie Mae said, following her instructions to bring him outside alone. She pulled close to Absolam. "I wouldn't be able to have a talk with you with them around." She cut her eyes their way. Absolam smiled and excused himself a moment to cross the floor and huddle with the men.

Soon, alone, they strolled along the building, Absolam following her lead.

"I've made the arrangements," he was saying. "Two hundred dollars I paid for you. I want to leave at dawn. You be packed and dressed and ready for me then."

She hesitated. This was what she had dreamt about. This was what she deserved. Maybe he wasn't the best looking man she had ever seen. Maybe he wouldn't even be a faithful husband, but he had wealth and she would be comfortable. And when it came time to let him have his way with her, well, she would pretend enjoyment the same as she did now with the paying miners. Still, she had accepted payment from another. Which would she betray?

The feel of the gold nuggets, hard against her body, made up her mind.

He didn't object as they moved away from the dance hall and deeper into the darkness.

"Where are we heading, little darlin'?" he asked, taking hold her arm and tugging her up tight against his chest. He turned her to face him and sought her lips. Cassie Mae responded, although she tensed with expectation for the stranger to make his appearance.

The kiss was long and when it ended, another was close behind. Kisses from smitten men were not unusual to Cassie Mae, actually very nice under normal circumstances, and after a few of them, she relaxed into Absolam's arms and allowed him a few fresh moves with his seeking fingers. Her eyes remained closed and she actually began to enjoy her experience and forget the stranger in the privy. Her arms wrapped around her suitor and her mind started to think again about what life would be

like if she went along with him. If he was willing to pay for her. The earlier dream of the white velvet wedding dress dangled like a star in her
mind.

She felt the violence in lieu of seeing it as Absolam was ripped away
from her grasp. He was sent falling to one side. In the moonlit fog, the
stranger stepped around Cassie Mae and stood high over the downed
man. He raised his arm over his head and as if in answer to a silent command, the fog cleared and the moon's light illuminated the scene.

"Mathuin!" Absolam cried.

"Are you ready, my mentor?" Mathuin screamed. "Are you ready to
take what I have to give you for what you have taken from me? Oh, I
have looked...searched many hundreds of years in the cities, in the
desert, in the continents, in the heaven's stars. You will not escape me
now, my teacher."

Absolam stared at his captor and his face took on a different mask,
that of rage, his eyes fairly glowed in the night. He jumped to his feet in
a swift, animal-like move, his gaze never leaving the stranger.

"A teacher to a willing pupil," he said, his voice more a growl than human.

"The hell you say." Mathuin stepped forward, his fists balled. "You
hunted for an innocent to make your pupil and you found me. You
took my life and then you took my eternity."

Absolam began a slow menacing circle around Mathuin. Cassie Mae
stared at him. He was different, his face that of an animal, the features
sharpened and sinister in the moonlight, his eyes blazing red and his
mouth open, revealing long snowy extensions that were no longer teeth
but fangs. And before her eyes, Mathuin lost the look of a human and
began to sprout long tufts of dark hair. Soon the two were circling her
with their eyes fixed only on each other. She began to scoot backwards,
hoping to go between them.

"I was living the life God gave me to enjoy," Mathuin said hoarsely.
"You had no right to take it."

"I gave you eternity, you stupid cur," Absolam growled. "You ran
with me a hundred years. How can you be angry now? And what are you
going to give me, as you said? A whipping?" He threw his head back and
howled. The sound split the night.

"No. Death," Mathuin replied. He jumped upon his enemy. His
hands were hairy claws and easily snagged through the other's coat of
fur, while his sharp incisors snapped at Absolam's throat. Not without a
fight did one give in and soon the two half-human beings were thrashing
about in the dirt with a viciousness Cassie Mae had never been subjected
to seeing before. She lay frozen in terror as the two slung blood and saliva through the air, some coating her dancing dress. Still she could not
move, only watch the two in their dance of death.

A movement to her right caused her to jerk forward. Two dark figures came toward them. One hand was outstretched and from it a sudden blue-tingled flame shot, disappearing inside the fight and stopping it as suddenly as it had started.

Absolam jumped to his feet. He kicked at the prone body of Mathuin. Absolam's two companions joined him. The three men picked up the body and disappeared into the dark.

Cassie Mae didn't wait to find out what would come next. She high-tailed it back to the dance hall where she spent the rest of the evening being twirled and wooed and handled like a straw filled doll.

There was no one to tell about what she had seen, certainly not the madam who would ship her off to the crazy house on the slightest excuse. One thing was certain; when the evening ended, Cassie Mae did not want to be alone. She clung to the first good prospect that came her way. He was a miserable old miner with bad breath and wild hair. He pushed a wad of dollars in her face and whispered his desire that she take him to her room. It wasn't until she started to undress that she felt the bag of golden nuggets. The realizations that it was true made her tremble and lose balance.

She stared at the ugly man waiting for her and also realized she didn't have to do this anymore. She had earned the gold. It was hers. She had delivered what was asked of her and it wasn't her fault if he had been destroyed.

"Get out of here," she whispered.

The miner stared at her as if she had lost her mind. His thin gray mouth parted into a tobacco stained grin.

"Who yer think yer're talking too?" He climbed from the bed and started toward her.

"Get out, mister. I don't want no trouble. Just get out. Here's your money back." Cassie Mae thrust the wad at him. He knocked her hand away before making a great lunge for her.

She stepped to the side and let the miner hit the wall. He howled and came after her.

She felt his breath on her neck, his bony fingers grasping her shoulders, his thin legs pressing against her, pushing her to the bed. She fought but he was too strong and managed to lay atop her until she could no longer breathe.

And then he was lifted away and she was free. Absolam threw the miner across the floor, breaking the door with the force of the throw. He took only a moment to gaze into her eyes before he slipped his hands under her back and legs and pulled her tight to him.

He glided through the window and she was floating along the forest floor still held securely against him.

There was no one to save her.

Downstairs many men waited. Cassie Mae preened in front of her mirror. Her eyes sparkled, her lips were a permanent rose blush, and her hair glistened in the lamplight.

She smoothed her red velvet dress and straightened her thick strand of black pearls. Her small black satin-enclosed feet tapped the floor.

Oh, how lovely she looked in her finery. Lovely enough to chose the one she wanted instead of praying he would chose her. Not that she gave a twit about any of them. They were no longer needed in her existence. She no longer wanted for anything. Her only desire now was to please him.

Every eye turned as she came down the stairs, her gloved hands extended for whichever man was quickest. There was a stampede to be the first.

"What's your name?" she asked the one.

"Richard Colley, ma'am."

"Well, Richard is the most handsome man here tonight, I believe," she cooed, weaving her spell.

"I would be honored if you would dance with me," he replied, blushing at her compliment.

"I'd be most happy to," she said and smiled.

He led her upon the dance floor.

"And, Richard," she whispered in his ear. "Maybe we could take a stroll out into the gardens later...say midnight when the moon is at its fullest."

"Oh, yes ma'am," he said.

As he whirled her past the windows, she caught a glimpse of three sets of yellowed eyes deep in the trees.

"Midnight, when we are the hungriest," she whispered at the window, then was swept away by his strong embrace.

Dweller On The Threshold

Michelle Scalise

As Margaret and I headed up the dark main staircase I wondered just how far she'd have to fall before her thick, pale neck would snap like an autumn branch. I envisioned her pearls bouncing along the wood floor as she begged for help, a thin trace of saliva pooling as she kissed the bottom stair. Engrossed as I was, it took a moment for the harsh knocking to break through my reverie. The servants had retired for the night so Margaret was forced to retrace her steps, mumbling angrily. She opened the door just wide enough for me to glimpse a stranger, his gloved hands clutching a large red book tightly to his chest. "Where does the Order meet? I must speak to your husband at once," the man demanded in a thick German accent and without introduction.

"Alfred is out for the evening," my stepmother explained. "You'll have to return tomorrow."

Though his attire was that of a gentleman, something about him unnerved me. His eyes strayed back and forth across the dark lawns as if he were hiding from shadows. The stranger's boots were covered in a thick dusting of dirt. He had arrived without horse or carriage.

I stooped to get a better look at whatever he might be searching for, drawing his attention. Startled by the sight of me he gasped and took a step back from the door as if my image were something seen in a nightmare.

Suddenly my vision blurred as if a thick fog descended the stairs and wrapped me in its white shadow. I caught a strange and yet vaguely familiar sulfurous scent in the air. Voices swam in a confusion in my head. I clutched the banister and listened to Daddy and the Order pleading for me to help them. It seemed as if they stood right next to me, all shouting at once in my ear. I closed my eyes and listened.

And then I understood.

This man cowering outside was the Dweller... and he was too late.

Margaret quickly closed the door.

"No," the stranger begged as he was pushed back. "Please Madame, I am working for your husband. I've spent hours out here searching for the right path to the gatehouse but I can't find my way."

The night was so quiet I could make out his words and yet he seemed to speak just above a whisper as if he feared the stars might overhear him. "I know all about the Order, Madam. I am their translator. I admire your caution but I can prove what I say. Look, I have brought the book."

Margaret lifted the folds of her drab grey gown, rose up on her toes and gazed through the small, diamond-pane window. The man waved his tome then quickly hid it beneath his overcoat. "The Order Of Arielis will all perish tonight if you don't lead me to the gatehouse."

Father always spoke of the Dweller with reverence. "He has powers to shield us from the spirit world," he explained. "There are few of his kind that exist on earth and we are lucky to have his guidance...though he does seem a little too cautious at times."

Margaret twisted the strand of pearls at her throat. "My husband belongs to a men's club by that name but that's all the information I can give you. Please...if you return tomorrow, perhaps?"

The man pounded at the door once more. "Is that what he tells you? A men's club?" Suddenly he began to weep loud, racking sobs.

I hated him for his weakness. Daddy never cried.

Margaret gazed up to where I stood like an expectant guest. "Sarah, go to your room." And then turned her attention back to the stranger. "Sir, leave at once or I shall be forced to get a servant and have you removed."

I knelt softly on the stairs, idly adjusting the lace of my gown until once more the Dweller's voice came slithering like a foul odor through the door. "You don't want to do that, Madame. The Order commissioned me to translate this book from the Teutonic language. I have worked day and night for months, turning over to them each page as I finished but...they should have waited until I had completed it. There are pages missing, knowledge they don't have. They'll never dominate the demon they've unleashed."

"Stop this at once!" my step-mother demanded. "I won't have you speak of my husband in this way. He is a good Christian man."

I stifled a laugh behind my hand as the stranger continued. "I can't save them from this. They don't know the third symbol to control it. We are all doomed because of your husband's folly. Soon it will come for me and when it is through it will take the rest of them into the hell they've played with."

Margaret turned to me once again, glaring. "Sarah, get the servants. Someone must still be up."

I came down the stairs softly, then stopped when I heard a deep growling outside.

I suspect the Dweller heard it too.

He called for my father, gazing out into the lawns at a massive, hunched-back shadow running toward the doors.

"Good bye, Dweller," I whispered.

"Alfred, they're coming," he cried. "In the name of all that's holy you must give me shelter. You brought them upon us all."

Margaret grabbed hold of the doorknob.

"That's probably his accomplice approaching," I said. " They'll wait until we open the door and then attack us. I've heard of such things happening."

Margaret looked back out the window. "But it doesn't look...human."

"I'm sure if Daddy were here he'd tell you this man is a fraud."

The beast charged as the Dweller begged to gods he'd never bothered to pray to. The door shook in its frame.

"My God!" Margaret yelled, backing away. "What is it?"

"Why don't you go find out?" I mumbled. "It certainly sounds hungry enough to eat two."

Why isn't she shrieking more? I wondered. Or pulling at handfuls of that unnaturally bright blonde hair? It's disappointing the way people never react the way one would expect.

Margaret returned to the window. "What have I done?" she was wailing. "Sarah, it's killing him."

"I think you should go up to bed," I said. "Daddy will straighten this out in the morning."

Margaret grabbed my hand, dragging me to the door. "Do you know what that thing outside is?"

The Order knew it was coming for them next. I could hear it in Daddy's broken voice drifting out of the woods.

Margaret shook me hard. "Why do they allow you to attend those meetings?"

"I'm not supposed to tell you," I said, pushing her aside to get a better view. Even on such a moonless night I could clearly see the brittle look of resignation on the stranger's face right before the snarling, dark figure tore out his throat. A thin sheet of his pale skin dangled from the beast's lips as if it awaited approval from its victim before continuing. The gleam of its swollen, silver-black haunches and its immense height reminded me vaguely of an Irish Wolfhound.

But I knew better. Margaret knew better too.

Pages from the tome the Dweller guarded beneath his black overcoat caught flight in the wind; swirling and floating skyward like dead leaves.

The voices of my father and the Order grew feeble and weak in my head, coming in waves of desperation. The beast wanted them to run, wanted the hunt as much as the kill.

For a moment the clouds parted, giving a clear vision of the animal's wide jaws working across the man's neck as if it were sawing a knotted piece of wood.

The Dweller's blood formed an accusing black path to our front door.

Margaret pressed her hands to her ears in a useless attempt to block out the sounds of bones cracking. "I have to know the truth." Her words came out in a half-whispered choke as if she were tangled in the drapery cords. The notion lingered as she grabbed my limp hand, dragging me from the window and down the dark hall into father's den.

A sputtering candle still burned at his writing desk, illuminating a family portrait that hung above the cold fireplace. In the painting Margaret perched on the edge of father's chair doing her best to look matronly. I stood behind them like a ghost.

"Sarah, hurry," she yelled. "We must get to the gatehouse and find Alfred." As she pushed open the French doors a gust of bitter wind lashed at my face.

"Margaret, you know Daddy has asked you never to interrupt his meetings. You wouldn't understand The Order."

Margaret glared. "What do the men do out there? Tell me!" Her nails dug into my shoulders.

I laughed, patting her parchment-dry, powdered cheek. "You've never asked Daddy, have you? Are you afraid of what you might learn, mother?"

"Don't ever call me that," she said, pulling the two of us out into the night in search of secrets.

My father always kept a carriage lamp on the steps to guide him home after his meetings and I grabbed it without losing a step. The wooded path was knotted with roots and thick weeds but I had traveled this way many times in the dark.

The men of the Order were silent now.

Normally I could manage the short walk to the cottage in minutes but with Margaret stumbling behind, reaching out for a handful of my gown as if I were her salvation, it took much longer.

"Tell me what is happening." Her quivering pleas amused me almost as much as watching her fall repeatedly on the upturned stones. "Is your father responsible for what I saw tonight?"

"You have nothing to fear, Margaret," I said, pulling my skirt away. The touch of her hands sickened me. "Daddy's a good 'Christian man'. You said so yourself."

"Sarah, wait for me," she cried, tearing her gown from the clutches of a dead bush. "I don't know the way as well as you do."

"Shhh..." I whispered. "Listen. I think it's following us now"

Margaret shrieked, wrapping her hands around my waist. "Alfred! Help me!"

I could smell her fear and the nauseating rose perfume she doused herself in.

"Daddy is always first because he is the leader."

Margaret stopped yelling and stared at me, forgetting for a moment the beast that followed us like a rabid pet. "What are you saying? I don't understand."

I forced her ahead of me, squeezing the back of her neck just enough to move her along. "They pray to Arielis, the dog-demon," I explained. "And that spineless man back there on our doorstep was their guardian. He kept them safe for a time."

"I don't believe you," she sobbed, trying to turn away till I pushed her further on.

"Daddy gave me to the Order. I am the sacrifice. For years he let me watch him with the other women, prostitutes I think. I didn't understand it then but he said when I was a little older I would be very special to the members. Now once a month I am brought out here to cleanse them in my blood. Remember how angry you were on my eighteenth birthday when he let me attend the meeting and we left you behind?" I sang softly. "Happy birthday to you, happy birthday dear Sarah."

Margaret spun and slapped me before I could stop her. "You are a liar and I'm going to tell your father every foul word you've spoken."

I smiled and firmly took her hand, forcing her to run as Arielis' howls filled the woods. "Hurry, mother. It would be a shame if the beast found you before we've seen Daddy."

As the stone gatehouse came into view Margaret hurried ahead, calling out to my father. At the stoop she froze, realizing that no light came from within. "My God! They've gone!"

I shook my head, laughing. "Trust me, they're waiting for us."

Opening the door carefully. "Daddy, look who came to visit." I had to drag my stepmother in behind me like a rag doll. The carriage lamp lit up every corner of the small room.

Margaret screamed and fell to the dirt floor.

Thirteen men swung gracefully by their necks from ropes knotted to the rafters. I figure they went in succession, each man climbing up like a convicted felon and sliding his head quickly through the noose then kicking out the seat for the next member to hurriedly take his turn.

Daddy's corpse was first because he was the leader. Face bloated and blue-black, his feet dancing heel-to-toe with their shadow. I sat on the bed and spun him round a few times like a hideous wind chime. "Arielis needs sacrifice."

Margaret shouted my father's name louder and louder as if he were suddenly hard of hearing and not dead. The low, insistent sound of a growl at the open door silenced her.

"All for you," I whispered to the beast.

The blood of the Dweller still dripping from the beast's lips as it sniffed the bodies one by one.

Margaret crawled into a corner like a spider assured of its imminent death.

I closed my eyes and lay back on the bed, smelling my father on the tattered quilt. Margaret's whimpers seemed to come from miles away as I raised my skirt and felt a cold muzzle thrust deeply between my legs. I reached up and grabbed Daddy's ankle, digging my nails into the frozen flesh of my sacrifice.

Landfill Dance

Stefano Donati

There she was. All alone at a booth near the back, sipping something with a white umbrella in it, just surveying the crowd.

No. Surveying him.

She couldn't be.

But long blonde hair, purple nails, breasts pouring out from her orange tank top. Thirty, thirty-two, something like that. Maybe, then. The woman who might know what had happened. Toby slid off the bar stool and tried to just wander casually toward her. But, three steps along, he had to speed up to hide the trembling in his gait.

She spoke first. "Pretty packed, huh?"

Oh, yeah, he thought.

"Did they have to card you?"

"Oh, I'm older than I look."

"Hmm. Twenty-one and three quarters, right?" She smiled, but at least not one of those smiles that said; Let's see if you can tell you're just wasting your time.

"You look..." The words almost skittered back down Toby's throat. "Well, you look tantalizing."

"And you sound like an English major."

"Hey, right!" He cringed. Compared to him, even a sophomore could sound like Super-Suave Man.

"It's okay," she said. "You feel awkward; I feel flattered." She patted the empty swath of leather beside her, and he revelled in the glimpse of thigh, even as a chill pelted his bones. His almost-brother was missing, likely dead. And this woman, if she was the woman, knew. Part of the story, anyway.

He sat next to her.

In a delicious purr, she said, "Those college girls must all have the flu."

"Why?"

"Because otherwise, they'd be swarming you. Can't say I'm complaining, though." At her words, he crossed his legs. "But you should really stay away."

"Vampire, right? Or married. Or a lesb..."

Christ, he thought. Clamp the mouth. You're as close to clever as you are to a clear career goal.

"None of the above," she said.

"What, then? Not my age, is it? Actually, I'm twenty-one and four fifths."

"No, not even your age." She swirled her straw all around the white umbrella. "You really want to hear this?"

"If it will help."

"Five men in the last eight months."

Okay, Toby thought; ask. She can't kill you for it, not in here. "Five men. What about them?"

"They disappeared. Five wonderful first dates, and then they disappeared." She gazed at him with wistful eyes. "Two are Missing Persons; the other three just haven't made the papers.

But they never called me, not after the first date — which went so well, they all did, weeks apart, laughs and hard confessions and this-could-be-my-mate thrills."

He squelched his sympathy, for now. Vinnie. "How, well, how exactly do you think they disappear?"

"I almost think I'm a carrier. A guy goes out with me, even just once, and then is doomed to thin and thin into oblivion." Her face was serious.

"You've seen that?"

"No."

"So why believe it?"

"I guess it's just easier than thinking that they..." She shook her rich, long hair. "Look, I'm sorry. You've caught me on a mawkish night. Five guys, though. Five first dates, and never more. Did they just abandon me? All the 'sit by the phone' stuff...well, I'm not that pathetic. But a dollop of romance now and then, is that so much to ask!"

"No, it isn't." He ached to just console her now, to promise they would solve these mysteries together.

But his best friend, and their good-natured debates about the virtues of westerns, Hemingway, the Lindbergh case. And now these slender legs, the long black hair. Promise nothing; promise everything.

Toby wiped sweat from his spectacles. All right. She was she; all the details matched the goddess Vinnie had praised to him through the bar's payphone. "Was one of these men Vinnie Cerasso?"

Great. Go sound just like frigging Dragnet.

She gaped at him. "You knew Vinnie?"

"My best buddy. You tell the cops about him disappearing?"

"They'd just say it's no crime for a guy not to want a second date. "

But it would be, thought Toby. Not to want a second date with her.

Could five men have all been so insane?

And, even then, where had Vinnie gone?

Toby said, "I read once about some guy who was struck by lightning seven times. Maybe it's like that with you. Three of the guys just skipped town, or had some weird tragedy, and the other two..." He stammered it out: "The other two were just plain nuts."

"You're sweet."

And Vinnie's dead, he thought. Vinnie wouldn't disappear on the whole world. Vinnie, the only adult classmate who ever cared about the trads. The only one who ever said so much as, 'Must be scary, being about to graduate.' The only one who agreed that even if you missed the Sixties, your anger over Vietnam could be sincere.

Dead. Toby tried believing he was just preparing for the body that would be found someday. But to really prepare, he'd have to give up hoping for Vinnie's safe return.

"I must sound stupid," she said. "All this talk about them disappearing. I should just get out of here."

"No."

"Why? Do you think you can find them for me? One of them, even?"

"Would they want me to?"

Of course they would, he thought; Vinnie most of all. He'd heard his buddy's rapture.

But she said, "Maybe you're right. I should just forget them." She sighed. "I know my theory's crazy, anyway. I mean, how could they blink into oblivion? I do wish they would, though."

"I understand."

"Well, it's stupid. Self-pity."

"No. Did you like them a lot? Did you like Vinnie?"

Hearing the name again, she winced. Toby saw that clearly.

"Didn't get the chance. But that's another reason I should leave; I might start really liking you."

His heart seemed to ram against his throat.

She sipped the last of her drink. "Look, thanks for your lightning theory. But five brief boyfriends vanished, that's more than just coincidence. If you don't want to blink out of existence, we should say good-bye right now."

Helplessly he watched her totter to the register, linger there while Barkeep Bob fished for change, rub her temples as if struggling to banish the curse she seemed so certain of.

Then instantly he was beside her, near the exit.

"No," she said.

"Listen. It doesn't have to be a long-term thing. Or really anything at all. But we could talk."

"Because you miss Vinnie, too?"

"For one thing, yes."

"And for another, I'm tantalizing. Right?"

"Well...yes."

"I don't want to be responsible for —"

"Wherever Vinnie went to, I can keep him company. Or else I can be with you. I mean, just to talk."

"So persistent." She looked him up and down, and his trousers tensed. "You're too young to be a cop."

"But not too young to be a friend."

Finally her hand extended. "I'm Kim."

He clasped it, and hoped his palm was not too moist. "Toby."

He opened the exit door and let her precede him into the warm spring night.

"I have my car," she said.

They walked to the sedan parked at the block's edge. She seemed to be shaking as much as he was. This time she opened the door for him, and he slid inside and sat gingerly beside her.

"You're sure?" She said.

Vinnie would never forgive him if he didn't, Toby thought. He would never forgive himself.

He had to try to find his friend.

"I'm sure," he said, careful not to brush her knee.

The engine roared to life and she guided the sedan lurching down street. "Let's go where it all began."

"Where what began?"

For a moment, her eyes seemed lost to time. "Last summer, by the landfill, I was nearly raped."

"The landfill past Hooch Pond?"

"Toby, did you hear what I just said?"

He could not look at her, not now. "Guess I just, guess I wanted to ease into it."

"He didn't. But I was saved anyway."

"Well, that's good." Jesus. Like she was talking about a tax refund or how nicely her azaleas were coming in this year. "By who?" He said.

"By whom, Toby. I thought you said you were an English major."

"Yeah, but we don't study grammar, or...so, what happened? I mean, as much as you want to tell me."

He looked at last, and saw tears streaking her moonlit face. But she did not say more, and he glanced to see an empty road ahead, and the sedan headed toward Hooch Pond. The landfill. His heart hissed dread. Don't make her have some crazy flashback. Don't make her shake her fists at the empty air the way Dad did.

That's one selfish fear, he thought, picturing the folks who had once shunned his dad. 'Don't sicken us with Vietnam talk, even if the talk's not half as bad as living it for two long years.'

The sedan creaked along the mud, closing toward the landfill dimly visible in the distance. Kim slowed, stopped, silenced the engine, and there it was: a heap of orange rinds and punctured mufflers and empty milk jugs and mildewed cardboard.

"Toby," she said, "it wasn't a who that saved me. You have to understand. It was a what."

"A what," he said.

"Here. Let me show you." She sidled out, and he swiftly joined her, his sneakers heavy against the caked mud.

"It really happened here?" He asked, not daring yet to use the word rape.

"And in the daylight, too. I was recycling my newspapers, being a good citizen, when this monster leapt at me from the side of his pick-up."

"I'm sorry."

"Toby. It's not your fault. And it could have been worse. We were all alone, it was a weekday, and he figured nobody else would come by for hours..." She reached the center of the landfill, and seemed to be searching. "It's stupid, but I kept thinking they would find the body."

"Body?"

"I told you I was saved."

He forced calm into his voice. "But not by who. By whom, I mean. By what."

"I couldn't tell you that until we got here."

Crickets split the night. The flap to a pizza box kept swaying to the wind's whispers. He stayed inches away from her.

"Don't be afraid," she said. "Just dance with me."

"Dance?"

"It's a beautiful night."

But the stench. He reeled back.

"Toby, weren't you secretly hoping a little we'd do more than just talk?"

"Well, maybe." He felt a bead of sweat trickle down his chin. "Mostly, I'm just sorry you got raped."

"We've gone through that: it's not your fault." She moved toward him, took his hands tenderly.

Here, amid the smells. Maybe, once upon a time, she had asked Vinnie, too.

"I've never been good at dancing."

"So we'll pretend. Here, Toby. Very good. Quite a gentle touch; you sure you're not a rascal with those college girls?"

"Um, quite sure."

"Now, keep facing me, and that way the what can smother you from behind."

He had to force his skull to register her meaning. But too quickly the what was upon him, slathering his skin with moist thrusts of what felt like chicken bones, and rotted bread, and shards of glass, and soiled diapers, and...

The landfill had come to life.

Gripping him too tightly to let him snare even a glimpse.

"Now," she said, "when God or whoever asks, not whomever but whoever, don't say I didn't warn you." She clutched his flailing, weakened hands and stretched them toward her to begin a waltz.

He felt his head yanked back, his arms yanked forward, darkness swimming through him...

"It saved me, Toby. It ate up every inch of him. You can understand why I'd be grateful, can't you? I mean, a meal now and then is the least I can —"

But he never heard the rest.

A Whisper From Behind

Beth Lewis

She sat quietly on her front doorstep, peering into the darkness of the night sky. She was thinking about the events earlier that evening, about her foster parents yelling at her for being twenty minutes late. She was sixteen and her curfew was nine o'clock. She'd slowly opened the door and tried to sneak in, but as she went to shut it a loud creak sounded and rang in her ears. Within a minute of her stepping into the house she was forced up to her room by the harsh, accusing words of her guardians. She'd lain on her bed and stared up at her plain white ceiling. Her foster parents hadn't let her repaint the room, or try to 'deface' it, as they regarded the room with sentimental value. The girl had no idea why, it was a plain white room, no posters, no features whatsoever, just a simple bed, wardrobe and desk.

Her previous foster parents had been two of the most understanding and generous people she'd ever had the good fortune to meet. They'd changed her; before she went to them she was a rebel, not wanting or needing anyone's help, but they changed her; they made her realize how good and kind people could be. She never wanted to leave them, never wanted to be replaced by someone more needy than herself.

Not wanting to dredge up painful memories she turned her attention back to the night. The giant blanket of darkness covered the sky as far as the eye could possibly hope to see. The veil of night strewn over the little houses, in their tight little rows with their white picket fences in the front gardens. Disgusted by their neatness, the girl stood up slowly, still looking at the blackness, and started to walk down her street towards the tiny shop on the corner and the two-screen cinema.

She'd gone no more that ten feet from her doorstep when that feeling set in, the feeling of being watched, from all angles, from everywhere. Her pace quickened, but still she felt that horrible wrenching in the pit of her stomach, more so than she did before. She tried to tell herself that no one was following her, and no one was watching her, but she wasn't convinced. The thoughts that she wished to stay in the back of her mind came forward, pushing their way to the front of the queue, taking over her mind. She glanced quickly behind her, but saw nothing. Her heart rate slowed down slightly and she began to regain her sanity, but the snap of a twig and a squeak of a new shoe from behind her rekindled her trepidation. Her unsuccessful attempts at trying to convince herself that nobody was there simply intensified her terror. She began to walk faster and faster, wanting to turn back to the safety of her house, but afraid of what was behind her, lurking in the shadows.

The houses were silent and shrouded in darkness, all their curtains pulled, and most of the lights off. She walked briskly past one with its curtains wide open, a roaring fire, and the flickering light of a television. She wanted so much to be in there at that moment, in the warmth, instead of out here in the bitterly cold night. The shadows made by the trees' skeletal limbs swaying and leaning in the wind heightened her feelings of unease.

She'd reached the end of her street, the silence was absolute, and there was not a soul in sight. That awful feeling of being followed still plagued her. Taking a quick look behind her and seeing nothing, she carried on walking down the street. The night air was cold on her bare face, the freezing fingers of darkness creeping down between her shoulder blades, making the hairs on the back of her neck stand on end.

The girl glanced at her wristwatch, turning it around on her goose-pimpled skin to view the face. Seeing that it was past ten, she remembered her curfew. Nine o'clock. How can they think anyone my age is supposed to have a social life with a curfew that early, she whispered to herself. These thoughts replaced the feeling of being followed. She noticed a man standing across the road from her, not moving, just standing stock-still, and apparently watching her. She turned away from him and walked at a lively pace, repeating over and over to herself that he wasn't there and he wasn't following her. The girl looked over her shoulder, the man wasn't where she'd seen him before, but was now on the same side of the road as her. His form was silhouetted by the street lamp that stood behind him, stretching up into the sky, trying to reach the heavens with its amber glow. When she saw him take a small step forward, the panic set in, and so did the rain. The tiny droplets beat down on her head like giant boulders; the sudden downpour had broken the deathly silence. She walked from street light to street light, not knowing where she was going and even where she'd come from, simply knowing that she had to keep walking.

Again she looked behind her; the man was following her, walking at the same pace as her and stopping when she stopped. He began to whistle a jaunty tune, obviously trying to make light of the situation. Instead, his actions increased her panic and made the moment almost unbearable. She turned from him and started to run down the rain-slicked pavement. He stopped whistling and she heard his heavy work boots thump against the street in her pursuit. The rain fell down sharply on her face and neck, the droplets running down her spine, making her shiver even more. Her teeth chattered together as the raindrops reached the small of her back, she felt as though a spear of ice was being dragged down her, piercing her skin and chilling her bones.

The man behind began to run after her, the sound of the steel-capped work boots getting louder and closer. She could now hear his laboured breathing, his quick breaths echoing in her mind as she ran faster and faster, turning into street after empty street in the futile hope of losing him. The rain stabbed at her face and hands, driving her on and on, faster and faster. Down the darkened alleyways where no sane girl would ever tread, yet he still followed her.

She ran down one alley that led back to her street, saw her house and hurried to the front door. She fumbled for her keys in her jacket pocket; finally producing them, she struggled to find the correct key, the rain blurred her vision, she tried to blink it out, but it kept coming back. She looked behind and saw the man standing at the open garden gate. Her heart hammered in her chest and she became short of breath, the man didn't move. He then walked slowly through the gate, closing it behind him.

There were a million and one thoughts running through her head at that moment, what was she going to do? What was he going to do? She at last found the right key but he was already half way up the garden path. She found the keyhole quickly, turned the key in the lock, shoved opened the door, and rushed in just as he put his right foot on the front step. She slammed the door on his gaunt, dripping wet face and looked through the door's small window. Within seconds, to her great relief, he had disappeared. Then she remembered the back door, and from some-where behind, she heard that same jaunty tune.

Mrs. South

Richard Gavin

The face that stared up at Graham Matherson from the paper seemed strangely familiar. Not the face exactly, but something the face represented. Something, an essence, one might say, that seemed to tug at a dark recess of his memory. The face was that of an old woman. Her eyes glared unblinkingly, dark as oil slicks. Her withered features were framed by a swirling mass of hair. Underneath her visage were two words, written in spidery, frantic letters.

MRS. SOUTH

Graham's eyes felt grainy and his right hand was afflicted with a searing pain. He had to pry his fingers apart to release the graphite pencil. He felt as though he'd been sleeping for days, though he had no memory of feeling drowsy, or falling asleep. The last thing he could recall doing was laboring over the notes on his family history, then, an instant later, he jolted awake. When he raised his head from the cradle of his folded arms he discovered that he had managed to sketch this strange portrait in his sleep.

Shaking his head clear, Graham plucked a Kleenex from the box and used it to wipe up the puddle of drool that had collected on his desktop.

The face of Mrs. South appeared just below his notes for the Matherson family circa 1700-1799. Chronicling the Matherson lineage was a pet project he'd undertaken to keep his mind occupied, but as his family's colorful history began to reveal itself, the notion of writing a book-length biography began to hold great appeal. God knew he could certainly use the money. Since Graham had resigned from the Ithaca public library he had been sustaining both himself and his ailing mother on what little funds he'd managed to squirrel away over the past few years. He was also forced to swallow a rather sizeable portion of his pride when he had to sublet his apartment so that he could move back into his childhood home in Orchard Park, New York. Cramming what little furniture he could into his boyhood bedroom was a bitter experience, as though the last fourteen years of his life were but a fantasy. As if the harsh world had forced him to recoil to the sanctuary of his youth.

If only it were that simple.

The sound of the ringing bell thrust the reality of the situation to the forefront of Graham's mind. He had installed the antiquated maid bell system four weeks ago, when his mother's health no longer afforded her the strength to call out to him. Now all she was required to do was tug on the silken cord that dangled next to the bed. The cord would rattle a small brass bell that hung from Graham's bedroom ceiling, beckoning his presence. The bell always seemed to ring at the least opportune times, but he never complained. If she passed away with his name on her lips, how could he ever forgive himself?

He pushed himself away from the desk and made his way to his mother's bedroom at the end of the hall. His movements were sluggish, for his limbs still tingled with pins and needles after being crouched in the same position for too long.

Mother had stopped ringing by the time Graham reached her bedroom door. The heavy drapery made the room's interior murky, almost sickly looking. He could see his mother lying beneath a bundle of quilts, her emaciated face resting upon the pillows. The cancer had been growing at such a rapid rate that it seemed to distort his mother's appearance with each passing day. He wondered if tomorrow he would find a stranger in her bed. He moved closer to her.

"You weren't napping were you? I'm sorry if I woke you, son," she said softly.

"No, ma. I was just doing a little reading. Is there anything I can get for you?"

She turned away from her son, unable to face him.

"I hate myself for asking you to do this again," she said.

Sorrow ripped at Graham's insides, but he refused to show it.

"That's what I'm here for, mom," he said. He slipped his arm behind the woman's neck, gently assisting her out of the bed, to the washroom. Her tiny body felt like a composite of chicken bones and tissue paper. Each time he had to lift her from the bed, Graham expected her to crumble.

He sat his mother on the toilet and politely looked away until she finished. Then back to bed he took her. She took a few sips of water from the glass and straw Graham held out to her before she drifted off to sleep. Graham remained in the ugly beige glow of the room for nearly an hour of silence before creeping back to his room.

Mrs. South's pencil-wrought visage greeted him from the cluttered desktop. Graham lowered his index finger to the paper and softly traced the circumference of her face before tacking the drawing to the wall at the foot of his bed. He was impressed by his latent artistic ability. The face was certainly lifelike. Haunting, just like the woman down the hall. Graham meditated upon his work for a few moments before going downstairs to prepare his supper.

He poured a can of tomato soup into a saucepan and heated it on the burner. As he stood over the stove, Graham's eyes were incessantly drawn to the stack of old mail that was piled on the kitchen table. All the envelopes were addressed to Mrs. Jodi Matherson. Most of them were overdue bills; a few were get well cards from distant relatives. The one letter that, to this day, angered Graham was from the local branch of Premium Med-Care, informing his mother that her medical coverage had been depleted. They told her very matter-of-factly that her late husband's health care plan could no longer provide her with the money she required for her cancer treatments. Graham had called the company, screaming at the witless phone operator until he was finally put through to a very officious-sounding woman who stated, "there was really nothing her company could do for him". Three days later his mother was released from St. Michael's Hospital. Graham took her home to ensure that her last days on earth were as comfortable as possible. Mother had said she was through with chemotherapy and morphine drips, she was happy to wither in the home where she'd raised her family.

She slept most of the time, occasionally requesting an aspirin to ease what must be abominable pain. Although his heart would grieve, there was a part of Graham that hoped this would all be over soon.

He took the soup back up to his room so that he might escape into his work. It was the one refuge he had left. He'd stumbled into the project quite by accident. It began by sifting through the mound of boxes that had been festering in the attic, evolving into an all-consuming pursuit to document his family's history. The boxes he carried down from the unkempt attic were filled with the usual paraphernalia - yellowed news clippings from local papers, faded photographs of nameless relatives, and a great deal of Graham's old school work. He eventually unearthed a battered leather satchel containing the hand-written memoirs of his great-uncle Phillip. Graham had stayed up most of the night absorbing his ancestor's recollections. Graham never realized that his family was in a direct line of descent from the infamous Mather clan of Massachusetts. His ancestor Cotton Mather had spearheaded many of the New England witch persecutions during the 18th Century.

Poring over all these books on geneology and New England history kept him grounded; at least until the bell rang again.

Graham pushed some of his notes to one side and set the steaming bowl down on the desk. Dusk leaked its pale light in through his bedroom window as though it was seeking shelter from the imminent nightfall. Graham perched himself upon his work stool and leaned forward onto his elbows. The dying leaves of the great oak tree made a sizzling noise as the autumn wind caressed them. Mrs. South's reflection seemed to be watching the leaves as well. Graham slowly turned his stool about. The woman's features were overlaid with the gnarled shadows of tree limbs that swept around her like cunning black serpents. If Graham concentrated enough, he could actually see Mrs. South breathing; see the muscles in her withered face stricken as she grinned, revealing the crooked rows of gray teeth.

He watched the shadows dance. Watched as they congregated below the hanging paper, as they entwined to form Mrs. South's limbs and torso. He stared in awe as the darkness bled down to create a pair of legs.

"Mother of Shadows, I praise thee..."

The words slipped free from his lips before Graham even realized he was speaking. A sense of self-disgust mushroomed up inside him. He ran a hand over his lips as though he could somehow cleanse them of the queer obscenity he'd uttered. His movements were those of an automaton as he quickly retrieved his pencil and moved toward the palpitating darkness. His hand seemed to vanish when he extended it toward the wall and began to trace the pencil tip along the rim of shadows. The task was done effortlessly, an exercise in automatic drawing. To Graham, it felt as though the sketch was being drawn by some other life form; something that was at once within and beyond him.

When the last detail was scratched onto the surface of the wall, the shadows seemed to scatter, restoring themselves to their proper niche of the moonlit room. Graham slid himself back along the floor to examine the fruits of his labor.

The silhouette trickled down the wall in a series of wavy pencil lines. They endowed Mrs. South with a gross parody of a body. The legs were almost comically disproportionate: one stout, the other lanky as an eel. Her outstretched arms were far too long for the flabby torso he'd drawn her. The sloppy, two-dimensional outline reminded Graham of the family portraits he'd drawn as a toddler.

Unable to pry his eyes from her, Graham remained hypnotized by the expressionist vision he'd created until exhaustion finally overcame him. He tossed himself onto the single-size bed and welcomed slumber.

It was still dark when Graham opened his eyes. Sweat beaded on his brow, his heart thundered in his chest. The details of the nightmare had already regressed to the labyrinth of his subconscious, leaving mortal terror in their wake. The house was quilted in late-night stillness. Nothing but the sound of the clock ticking from the living room; slowly, inexorably, like a metronome keeping rhythm for some otherworldly song. Graham wiped the sweat from his face and breathed deeply. Part of him was straining to remember the dream; the other was struggling to repress it.

He could remember fire. And screaming. A great deal of screaming. Some of the cries were those of young children, but the majority of the voices were women's. The details of the nightmare then began to trickle their way back into his conscious mind. Although Graham did not wish to relive them, his psyche continued to assail him with the horrible images.

He had been in the dream, tramping through a field of scorched earth that was littered with shards of charred bones. There were other figures there as well, some of them strangely familiar.

She had been in the dream. There could be no mistaking those pitch black eyes that glared at him through the flames. The old woman was lashed to the trunk of an oak tree. Kindling had been piled around her ankles and a group of faceless individuals touched their blazing torches to it. The fire swelled and the crowd cheered. The woman that was tethered to the tree stared at Graham, stared *into* him. Guilt jabbed at his insides as he watched helplessly. The crone remained silent, as if to spite her persecutors. It was not until the flames engulfed her completely that the woman opened her mouth. Not to scream, but to laugh.

Graham shuddered. In the darkness Mrs. South appeared to be blinking. Her tiny mouth opening and closing like a beached fish. Was she trying to speak?

'A trick of the light,' Graham thought to himself, until he saw her move.

The sketch began to pry itself from the surface of the wall. The plaster ballooned outward, fleshing out the woman's preliminary pencil form. Mrs. South's eyes never left Graham's. Slowly his astonishment evolved into a strange desire. He wanted her to be free, to be real, to be near him. One leg popped free, then the other. An arm. Her face.

The old woman advanced. Graham could hear the shallow breath escaping through her gaping mouth. Her movements were wobbly and awkward; like an actress in a silent movie. Her misshapen legs somehow managed to carry her across the bare wood floor. Wisps of hair hung before the furrowed skin of her face. Closer she came. Closer. Graham lay paralyzed, fearing that the slightest movement would shatter the miracle he was experiencing.

Mrs. South pressed one knee down onto the mattress. She leaned forward. Graham's nostrils were attacked by the odor of scorched flesh, but he did not care. She was near him now and that was all that mattered.

"Mother of Shadows," he hissed, "I worship thee."

Mrs. South was arched over him now, her breasts dangling like withered fruit, her bloated belly pressing against his. She exuded an otherworldly presence, a spirit far too great to be imprisoned in a mortal carcass. Graham closed his eyes, his loins now livid with desire.

The bell clanged as Jodi Matherson feebly tugged the silken cord. It startled Graham into awareness. He opened his eyes in time to see Mrs.

South leaking back into the wall, her figure melting into the flat, motionless outline. A cold feeling of loss washed over him. The bell rang again.

Graham leapt up from the bed and fled to his mother's room. She was sitting upright, her spindly arms extended, her mouth twisted in a look of disgust. She'd been sick again. Graham rushed to her and helped her remove the soiled nightgown. He balled up the quilt and top sheet, tossing them into the laundry hamper.

She sat there like a macabre marionette on the bed. Not speaking to her son as he collected a wash cloth and filled a bowl with warm water. Graham wiped away the mess while his mother focused her bulging eyes on nothing at all. It was the first time he had ever been afraid of his mother, of what she was becoming.

Graham slid a clean nightgown over her head and reclined her back onto the pillows.

"I bet this feels better," he said as he laid a clean quilt over her. Jodi continued to stare.

It was nearly four a.m. by the time Graham returned to his room. He knew that sleep was out of the question, so he part hunched himself over his desk and began scouring his books of his family's history.

He salvaged a dog-eared paperback entitled *Purged of Sin: Being a History of Witch-Hunts* from one of the boxes and began thumbing through the musty-smelling pages. Several passages had been underlined in pencil, undoubtedly by a relative, for they were the ones that discussed Cotton Mather and his persecution of New England "witches".

Of all the covens in Massachusetts, it read, *the one headed by a mysterious old witch known only as Mrs. South was the most feared and reviled. Rumored to have taken her name because of its connotation of Hell – the Underworld where she claimed to draw her power, Mrs. South was considered by her followers to be an earthly vessel for "the great Shadow Mother", or "the Goddess of the Abyss". Mrs. South guided the young witches in her coven through strange nocturnal rites. It was believed that many local men were also lured to this Sabbaths, only to suffer degradation, torture and murder at the hands of the demonic women. Finally, in May of 1776, Cotton Mather stormed Mrs. South's hovel and dragged her to the nearby woods where she was immediately sentenced to death by fire. This was the only execution in which Mather personally assisting in setting the victim ablaze.*

Graham shuddered, closed the book. Mrs. South's gaze had never seemed so malevolent.

As dawn broke the darkness with streaks of orange light, Graham was unable to purge himself of the irrefutable notion that today would be the last day he would ever see his mother alive. Even before he entered that grim room to look upon her languished form, he knew she was at

Death's door. He spent the morning at her bedside, rarely even thinking of Mrs. South.

Jodi remained silent throughout the day. She did not drink, nor did she move. She simply stared – her eyes as vacant as those of Mrs. South. No, perhaps even more vacant, for these sickly globes did not shift with shadows as the old witch's had. These were cadaver's eyes; eyes that had seen what the future holds and now waited complacently for the body to accept its inevitable doom.

At dusk Graham brought his mother two aspirin and a glass of ice water. Neither of which she accepted. Then, apropos of nothing, she reached out and clasped her tiny hand around his. For that fleeting moment, the woman was familiar to him, as though she had peeled away her death mask to offer him one last loving glance. But as quickly as it had come, the moment vanished. The waxy visage was restored and his mother fell back into a shallow sleep.

Graham rose and made his way to his bedroom. Night was once again blossoming outside, dappling the room with a soft, dream-like glow. He shuffled to the window, hung his head and began to weep, striving to convince himself that it was for the best. The form of Mrs. South flashed through his mind.

'As one body withers, another blooms,' he thought, though he was unclear as to what it meant.

He felt the hand upon his shoulder and it turned his blood to ice water. In the window glass Graham saw the reflection of Mrs. South, standing behind him, her bleached and sagging body inching closer to him. He whipped around, recoiling from her clammy touch. The old woman pressed the dry tip of her finger to his lips then coiled her arms about him. Graham gasped. The woman's torso felt like a water-filled balloon: rubbery, almost malleable to the touch.

She began to whisper to him. Her words sounded like gibberish to his ears, but were effective in stirring emotions deep inside him. Graham probed the depths of those alluring, ancient eyes. He wanted her. Needed her. The two of them began to move about the room in a perverse dance that began slowly, but quickly intensified.

An inferno of desire began to rage inside Graham. Each movement made her body feel that much more real. The two of them spiraled about the room, knocking over furniture, toppling the books of Mather family history. Graham watched in amazement as Mrs. South breathed on one of the volumes, causing the book to be consumed by emerald flames. The green fire raged between them. Ashes of Cotton Mather's obscenities curled black and took part in the dance, flitting through the air like chaotic moths. The dance continued. Screaming. Laughing. Babbling and turning widdershins. Mrs. South tore at his clothing. He sighed when his naked flesh pressed against hers. Round and round. The tremendous feeling of dizziness caused strange colored shapes to splatter before Graham's eyes. And although he did not want to stop, his body toppled to the littered ground.

Mrs. South came down with him.

"Mother of Shadows, I am thee."

She was upon him. Graham moaned with bliss as her warm wetness engulfed him. He clutched at her warm and vital body. He felt the blood of the ages gushing through her. As they ravaged one another, the green fire cracked and the room span. Graham could feel himself beginning to climax. Bells rang inside his head. Shadows began to seep into the corners of his eyes, blackening his surroundings until there was only he and the Mother of Shadows straddled over him. His fists clenched, head reeling, Graham was suddenly overcome with the notion that he was copulating with all women and with the one Woman. The one true Woman whose cleft is the night sky and whose womb is the Void of non-being. They were like some eager, atavistic Adam and Eve, lost in a wanton garden of earthly delight.

Fire and flesh and blood and bells and whispers.

Graham's muscles tensed as he spent himself inside her.

Instantly the world was bright, silent and restored. He opened his eyes.

The woman that was draped over him felt cold. As Graham brushed away the mass of sweaty hair, he shrieked. Screamed with both revulsion and disbelief.

His mother lay sprawled on top of him; her tiny body still attached to his. Peripherally Graham noticed her limp hand still held the silken cord of the maid's bell. He peeled her corpse away as though it were burning him. Shivering, consumed by dread, Graham stood amidst the debris of his mother's bedroom. Bed sheets, water glasses, papers. The litter spread down the hallway, into his room.

He stormed into his room, which was now tainted with the odor of burnt paper. And burnt flesh. The wall at the foot of his bed was blank. Graham reached out his hand, touched the cold, smooth plaster. A blank sheet of paper remained tacked to white plaster.

From somewhere below him there rose a laugh that was both spiteful and jovial. Bursting from the bedroom, Graham ran down toward the source of the laughter.

When he reached the main floor of the house, he found the front door open. Dead leaves blew into the front hall.

An autumn wind chilled Graham's naked flesh as he stared out at the vacant, moonlit street.

No More A-Roving

Lynda E. Rucker

The Seagull Hostel wasn't mentioned in Paul's battered copy of Let's Go, but the Australians he'd drunk with back in Cork had recommended it to him, as had his last lift across the Dingle Peninsula. Now dusk had come and gone and a good Irish mile or two out from town he'd begun to wonder if he hadn't been misled. The wind and the chill rain had redoubled their efforts against him, and the couple of cars out on the roads had flown past him in a spray of water. The backpack had seemed so light the first time he'd packed and hefted it. Now it sat like a ton of bricks across his shoulders and lower back. Perhaps he should hike back into town, before it got too late, and blow his budget on some cramped, overpriced bed and breakfast; but there it was, after all, a signpost pointing him down a muddy lane to a rambling wooden structure. In the dark of the night it was merely an outline. It looked deserted.

Paul swore under his breath as he approached it, but just as he was stepping up onto the porch the door swung open before him. "Come in, love, you'll catch your death," and the dumpy middle-aged woman was pulling him in out of the elements. Paul's eyes took a few minutes to adjust to the room before him: hostel-sparse and dingy, a few old chairs and a black and white television in one corner playing the theme to a soap opera, sunny Australian voices ringing incongruously across the gloom.

"Awful night for it," the woman commented needlessly. "Lucky you weren't knocked down by a car with no moon out there. Will you be wanting your own room or a bed in the dormitory, then?"

"Dorm," he said. He'd get a night's sleep and head out in the morning. The Seagull, he realized now that he'd finally found it, was too far from town to suit him. Even a trip to the pub would require him to slog back through that endless wet rainy night. Hadn't the Australians described it as being closer in? Perhaps the name hadn't been the Seagull at all, perhaps the Seabreeze or the Seaview. He might have missed his intended destination entirely in the storm. All the same he might find someone interesting to talk to here, even a travelling companion.

"Right, dear. Six pound fifty. I'm Mrs. Ryan and my girl Laura works from time to time too. Kitchen's through that door there." She pointed. "We don't lock you out during the day, but we ask that if you'll be staying you'll let us know by noon."

Wandering past her, down a short passageway and into the kitchen, he saw why he'd thought the place deserted. All the lit rooms were here at the back. Two girls sat giggling at a rough wooden table in the bare narrow room, spooning yoghurt from tiny Yoplait containers. Paul lowered his backpack gratefully to the floor. He nodded at them and they giggled in return.

"I'm Paul," he said, "what's your names?"

They were from Cork, they told him, come here for work. Day in, day out, they gutted fish at one of the warehouses. Seventeen years old and their faces were hard and flat, their accents so thick he had trouble understanding them. Their complacency depressed him. When he wasn't directly addressing them, they whispered to one another and giggled more. At what, he wondered; his relentless American desire to strike up a friendly conversation? In the last year he had learned that things about himself that he had long imagined to be the very essence of Paul-ness were in fact culturally concocted mannerisms. The discovery was troubling, as though something vital had been stolen from him.

At last he got to his feet and retrieved his backpack, meaning to retreat to the dormitory. If no one there proved worth talking to either, at least he could read for a while before he went to sleep. Reading would distract him from thoughts of Alyssa; she'd stood him up in Scotland where they'd planned to catch the ferry to Ireland together. He'd even stayed two extra days in Stranraer, dull port town, waiting for her to arrive. Somehow, her behaviour, though unexpected, hadn't surprised him. Presumably she'd gone on ahead of him, was most likely somewhere in Ireland still. Had he been Alyssa, he wasn't entirely certain he'd have waited on himself either; the real surprise was that she'd not ditched him earlier. And now he'd been travelling so long he found himself running out of reasons not to go home.

The dormitory was at the end of the hallway, past some doors he assumed were private rooms. Stocked with eight bunk beds, it was deserted save for a large young man snoring atop one. The bare walls and windows threw the harsh overhead light back at him. A door at the other end, open slightly to the outside, concealed the couple on the other side of it, a male and female speaking something that sounded like German, or maybe it was Dutch. The scent of hashish drifted languorously across the room.

Paul chose the bed farthest from the snorer to dump his pack. Something he'd seen earlier, in the reception room, worried at the back of his mind. Something he'd noticed, and he couldn't put a name to it.

He was too tired, and exhaustion was playing tricks on him.

He backtracked to the bathroom, a cavernous cold place, to change into dry clothes for sleeping, and brushed his teeth under a bulb that made his face look sickly and orange. So complete was the quiet and sense of isolation that he jumped when the door swung inward and a yellow-haired boy strode past to the urinal.

Paul heard voices in the passageway as he gathered up his shaving kit. They were still hanging around outside the dormitory room when he stepped into the hallway. Four of them, two girls and two younger-looking guys, their voices loud and edgy and frayed by alcohol and cigarettes. Paul found that all at once he didn't feel sociable any longer. Another moment and they were joined by the yellow-haired boy. Paul pushed past them and they gave him the indifferent glances of a well-established travellers' clique.

Another body had occupied the lower bunk opposite Paul's, a small form entirely hidden under the comforter save for some ginger curls strewn across the pillows. Paul rummaged in his backpack for one of the paperbacks he'd picked up in Dublin.

But the book bored him. He let it slide to the floor and rolled over, shutting his eyes against the glaring light overhead. He thought of home; it was like swallowing bile. Things would look better in the morning. As sleep overtook him, the something unremembered worried at the edges of his mind. Something he'd seen when he first came in, and only now had begun to realize the significance of. Sleep claimed him before he could sort it out.

He was awakened by the sound of a child crying. He opened his eyes to a room gone dark, and lifted his head before he realized the sound was that of the wind. He got up quietly, taking care not to irritate the vocal springs of the sagging bunk bed as the slow breath of sleepers rose and fell around him. There seemed too many of them, from the sound of it; only eight bunk beds and not all of them filled, but so many different breaths. A recollection of waking earlier, too, stirred in him, a memory of someone clambering onto the top bunk above him, but the bunk was empty, its bedding smooth. Stealing over to the window Paul saw that the rain had stopped and the sky partially cleared; the wind blew heavy, fast-moving clouds across a moonlit sky. Under the sound of the wind the sea crashed, closer to the hostel than he'd realized. His own breathing fell into a rhythm with it. His eyes adjusted—indeed, the sea lay just beyond, moonlight glinting off the water. Paul leaned closer, pressed his face against the glass as if that might aid his vision. Surely he imagined the tiny boat on the water, manned by several figures, mere silhouettes in the moonlight. A rowboat. And somewhere out to sea, a distant glow, as if a lighthouse on some long-deserted island kept its covenant to beam would-be sailors to safety. Yet no one would dare that cold wild sea, even in daylight, in such a craft. A second possibility occurred to him: perhaps they were in trouble, perhaps there'd been some accident at sea and their vessel had sunk, and Paul was the only person in the world who could rescue them now. His gaze roamed wildly round the room as though he might find help there, wishing he'd never awakened, wishing someone else had spied the boat. He must have mistaken some trick of the moonlight. He would have to go outside, get closer, to be certain.

He felt his way along the wall till he found the door that had sat ajar earlier in the evening. He pulled hard on it, but it did not budge. Paul ran a hand over the knob, looking for some lock to be twisted, and above it in search of a deadbolt. Nothing. The surface of the knob and door were utterly smooth, yet as he tugged on the handle he felt not the slightest give.

Panic settled over him like a dream. Back to the window. He must alert someone. But who? Would he wake someone in the room, race to the reception telephone and phone the local police?

But he no longer spied the boat. A trick of light, indeed. He scanned the surface of the water, uncertain of what he was looking for. Sometimes, when he was very tired, dreams lingered like after-images. Surely that had happened tonight.

The stillness closed round him again. Something in the hostel was not waiting, not waiting for anything at all. He returned to his bed where sleep came much later, and troubled.

The next sound that awoke him was that of the heavy boy gasping his way through a round of callisthenics. In the harsher morning light—for the day dawned like slate—he saw that the boy was more of a man, at least in his late twenties or early thirties. The boy-man wore the clothes of someone even older, clothes Paul associated with the middle-aged or elderly—white undershirt, boxers, black socks pulled up to his knees. The man was trying to touch his toes. He bent at the waist and bobbed up and down. Paul closed his eyes again. His watching might be intrusive. When he opened them again, the man stood over him, sweating.

"Name's David," he said, sticking out a fat, sweaty palm for Paul to handle. "Welcome to the Seagull. Did you just come from Dublin?" He was English.

"Paul," Paul said, though he didn't offer his own hand in return.

David remained undaunted. "On holiday, are you? From America?"

Paul looked past him for the group from the previous night, or the German couple. But he and David were alone. It must be later than he realized. He was very tired. He'd been traveling so much lately. It might be good to stay another day or two and rest.

"Never really had any interest in going to America," David said. "Like it here." He depressed Paul in some unaccountable way. "You at university?"

"Yes," Paul said. He started to offer more, but offering more led to conversation. Paul did not want to converse with David.

When he was able to escape, he located Mrs. Ryan and told her he'd be staying another night. He was shocked to see by the clock behind her that it was almost noon. Mrs. Ryan looked irritated, as if in waiting she'd had to turn away a bevy of travellers clamouring for his bed.

He showered and took a walk out the back of the hostel and down near the water. He found the coastline here forbidding. The green tree-less landscape led right up to the edge of the sea, a sheer drop; to the south climbed a rocky cliff. Cold sea spray stung his face. He thought he saw two figures through the fog, clambering up the cliff. Perhaps the German girl and her boyfriend. He shouted after them. After all, they were staying there together, and it was perfectly permissible, expected, even, to strike up a conversation under such circumstances. But they either ignored him or didn't hear, though the girl did turn once and stare at him, hair whipping about her face, before turning back to follow her boyfriend further up and out of sight.

The beacon he recalled from the night before managed to penetrate the mist with a soft yellow glow. A lighthouse, perhaps, on some rocky, craggy island off the coast here? He would ask Mrs. Ryan about it later. If the light he'd seen was real, had the boat been as well? The dinghy caught his eye, then, drawn up to the shore below though he could see no way of getting down to it. Seeing it there surprised him; he'd have imagined that at some point high tide would obliterate the narrow stretch of beach, making it a gamble to leave anything there. And the choppy sea seemed hardly an ideal waterway for the poor craft. Paul shivered against the chill, and in the next moment recalled his dream of the night before. And certainly it had been a dream. Otherwise, the people he'd seen in the boat had been lost at sea, their tiny boat washed ashore. And it would have been his fault. He tried to imagine it, adrift on that icy ocean, perhaps for days; perhaps worried that to come too close to the rocky cliffs dotting the shorelines there would break the boat up entirely, smash it against the rocks.

His imagination was getting away from him again.

Later today he'd trek into town and pick up a few things to eat and see about bus connections to Tralee and Limerick, anyplace east of here. He'd had enough of the countryside; enough of the coast, and this seemed less like a restful way station and more like a place where weary travellers went to die. Something crawled down his spine at the thought, surprising him. *Something just walked over my grave.* Paul stuffed his hands in his pockets and turned his back to the sea, but the chill still stung at the tips of his ears, the back of his neck, needling his skin.

"That's Alyssa's scarf!"

Paul didn't think he'd meant to speak out loud. He'd been watching television in the lobby; wrapped in his jacket against the chill he hadn't noticed when he arrived the night before. But the thing that had bothered him the previous night dawned on him now; it was the soft grey woollen muffler snug against Mrs. Ryan's throat. How many times had he seen Alyssa wrap it round her own beautiful neck?

"What, love?" Mrs. Ryan, propped before a tiny space heater with a magazine, looked over at him.

Paul recognized it as though it were a beloved article of clothing belonging to him, the black threads woven throughout the grey in a checkered pattern, the edges frayed because the scarf was old and Alyssa had loved it too much to throw it out.

"Did someone leave that here?" he asked. "The scarf, I mean?"

Mrs. Ryan looked confused. "My scarf?"

"Yes, I think it belongs to a friend of mine." Impatient. Alyssa might somewhere close by. She might have left only just before he arrived. She might have said where she was going. What he would say to her if he caught up to her, he would not think about.

"Why, no, that's impossible. My husband, God rest his soul, gave me this one Christmas—oh, six, seven years gone now it is. Keeps me warm as can be."

"Did a girl named Alyssa stay here in the last week or so?" Paul demanded. Angry now, he tried to control his tone. She was lying. "It's—I need to get in touch with her. It's very important to me to know if she's been here."

"You're the first new guest I've had in a while," Mrs. Ryan told him placidly. He could hardly accuse her of anything, could he? He could hardly tell her outright that he knew she was a liar. Paul's hands curled into fists and he shoved them deep in jacket pockets. Cheap old bitch. Wouldn't heat the place properly and stole from the guests. And he hadn't made it into town to check on bus connections after all. Well, tomorrow, he'd just leave. He'd get up early and go and sometime during the day he was bound to catch either a bus or a lift out of town.

Paul pushed himself up from the chair and without another word to Mrs. Ryan stalked down the hallway to the dormitory. The group he'd encountered the night before were apparently out again, as was the German couple. The form on the bed opposite his was still there, but this time the covers were thrown back to reveal a small face beneath the ringlets. Paul noticed a bottle of vodka peeking out from the girl's backpack.

Perhaps he'd try walking into town now. The night had cleared, and it wouldn't be such a bad walk as long as it stayed that way. He might even talk to someone about bus schedules. He asked David about a good pub.

"Try O'Flaherty's," David suggested, and Paul realized with a sort of horror that David was preparing to accompany him. The thought of the pub immediately lost its appeal, and he began fumbling over excuses as to why he wasn't really interested in going tonight, especially. David, undaunted, took off for town, wearing a heavy overcoat and good boots. Soon after Paul began to wish he'd accompanied him after all. He had no wish to return to the reception room to watch television with Mrs. Ryan, and the German couple returned but spoke in low voices with one another. Paul didn't remember falling asleep atop his covers with all his clothes on, and he didn't wake again before morning.

The rain started again soon after he got up, and he couldn't see heading out to hitchhike or wait for a bus in that weather. Anyway, he'd over-slept again.

He boiled instant coffee in a deserted kitchen and later made his way out back again to the sea. He looked for his fellow travellers again, per-haps on the cliffs, but saw no one. He smoked the cigarettes he'd bummed from David and threw the butts into the ocean. A bitter wind blew across the water, and somewhere through the mist the beacon shined for someone. He thought of the fishermen who made their liv-ing from this sea, of the thousands upon thousands dead of blighted po-tatoes, years of famine scarring this green harsh land, and he thought of America. The more he thought of it the more it seemed to him to exist someplace very far away. He wondered if he crossed this sea if it would be there any longer. He wondered if he cared.

He strode to the edge, where he'd seen the dinghy below. The strip of shoreline remained, but the dinghy was gone.

It crossed his mind that perhaps it had broken free from its moorings somewhere, drifted up on the tide here and then back out again, but that hardly seemed likely. There had been a deliberateness about its placing on the shore below, as though someone had pulled it in from the water and carefully placed the oars crossways inside of it.

He asked Mrs. Ryan about it that night in the reception room, but she shook her head. "Oh, love, it might be anybody's. Still some fishermen in these parts, you know. We're not all in the business of providing warm beds for tourists." But who would row a dinghy on that wild sea? And there were no lighthouses off shore around here, she assured him, she was certain of that. As she spoke Paul couldn't keep his eyes off that muffler round her neck. He was wild to get hold of it. He'd remembered how to be sure: something he'd teased Alyssa about. She'd written her name on the tags of all her clothes like a child going away to summer camp: Alyssa Meiers. It was an oddly homey and endearing move from the usually elusive, too-beautiful-to-be-true girl. Not the kind of girl who usually fell for Paul. Not the kind of girl he could expect to wait for him to catch up now. And the two of them, together, would have always been that way: Alyssa, far ahead, and Paul, lagging behind, trying to reach her.

In the kitchen he cooked up some packaged noodles and ate them in front of the television. The ginger-haired girl made an appearance outside of her bed at last. She said her name was Rosie and she was from Melbourne. He wondered why she kept getting up and leaving the room until he realized she was refilling her Pepsi can with alcohol. Her speech became slurred and she stumbled once across the rug at the threshold, and she tried to laugh it off but she looked like she was crying. Then she left the room again and didn't come back. Paul was glad. He waited until he was pretty sure she'd gone to sleep, or passed out, and made his way in there as well.

In the morning another girl kneeling beside Rosie, trying to wake her, roused him from sleep instead. "Ah, Rosie, did you have too much to drink again?" the girl was saying, her voice a pleasing Irish cadence, and Paul caught sight of Rosie's face, screwed up tight against the morning like a little girl's, fists rubbing shut eyes. He rolled over and tried to sleep again.

But, "I don't want to go," Rosie whined, "the others have gone and I don't want to go after them."

"There, shhh," the Irish girl whispered as though she were soothing a small child. "No need to fret about it." Later, Paul found the girl in the reception area. This was Mrs. Ryan's Laura, then. She was checking in the first new guest Paul had seen since he arrived, a tall, heavy-set blonde girl.

"Did a girl named Alyssa Meiers stay here before I came?" Paul asked Laura, hoping she'd be more receptive than her mother.

"Oh, I'm sure she didn't. I've a good memory for names," Laura assured him. He watched her as she spoke, looking for deception beneath her cheerful ease.

The blonde girl said, "You looking for somebody? She'll turn up sooner or later. That's what happens you know, you think you've said goodbye to somebody forever and you run into them three or four more times over the next couple months." She had the accent-less voice Paul had come to associate with Americans from the west coast, and sure enough, she hailed from California.

"I've been travelling eighteen months," she told him as they shared a cigarette in the kitchen. "My friend was with me for a while, but she was raped in Spain. Hitchhiking. She went home after that. Before that we went all over Thailand, Malaysia, Nepal . . . you been to Southeast Asia?"

Paul said he hadn't.

"Man, that is a trip. Like, you wouldn't believe the drugs you can get there. And cheap! We stayed there a really long time, cause everything was cheap. Ireland costs too damn much."

Paul was taking a dislike to the girl, her coarse and abrasive manner, and her bulky body. "When are you going home?" he asked, because somehow he felt the question might hurt her and he wanted to do just that.

She stopped, drew in a long drag of smoke and shrugged. "Dunno. Why would I want to do that?"

And so it went. "How long have you been staying here?" Paul asked Rosie once, and she just shook her head again and wouldn't talk to him anymore, just stared at the television as though mesmerized by the opening credits of a variety show. He dug through his address book but couldn't find the slip of paper where he'd written down the name of the place the night it had first been suggested. Perhaps it had been the Seashell, or the Albatross, in which case he was here under false pretences. He said it to himself as a joke and didn't feel like laughing afterwards. If he wanted to stay in the area, it wasn't as though he had to remain here. He could ask around in town, perhaps get to the bottom of it, find the other, more pleasant hostel, which he must have mistaken this one for. Surely no one would recommend this place to anybody.

For a long time no one arrived or left; and he eventually decided the five travellers he'd encountered the first night were long gone, for he never saw them again. The German girl and boy spoke only to one another, even avoiding eye contact so it was impossible to strike up a conversation naturally. Late one morning he caught sight of them climbing the cliffs again. He could catch up to them; perhaps they'd been here long enough to remember Alyssa. They could hardly avoid him when it was only the three of them in that deserted landscape. And he was lonely. The other visitors depressed him.

The cliffs were slick and dangerous, sprayed with seawater. The couple were far more sure-footed than he. He clambered across the rocks, ignoring caution; curiosity rendering him careless, and still kept them barely in sight. At last they seemed to slow a bit, so he was able to pick his way more carefully. A glorious view awaited him. Even in the gloom, or perhaps because of it, the seascape spread before him bespoke a beautiful desolation. It was in one of those moments, gazing about him, that he nearly lost them again.

They had turned down a track, though, a path down the cliff. The way looked even more treacherous than the one he'd taken here. Paul might be able to follow them down, but he couldn't imagine making his way back up again. For a long moment he stood watching them, helplessly. He realized that if they continued as they were going they might reach the stretch of shoreline, if indeed it were possible to reach it at all.

Surely that wasn't safe. The tides came in swiftly. They might be trapped, cut off; but his concern was not great enough to send him after them. Cowardice, he supposed. He winced as he thought the word, however accurate it might be. It was a trait he'd been able to conceal from Alyssa in the short time they'd known each other. It was just as well he'd lost her; she'd have found him out anyway.

Paul waited until the couple re-emerged on a narrow rocky spit of shoreline further to his left. Until now, he had not noticed the dinghy drawn up on the dry land there. The two of them shoved it off into the water, and the boy clambered in first, then helped the girl in. They both began to row, out toward sea. Away toward the light that beamed feebly but steadily somewhere in the mist.

Eventually he lost track altogether of how many days he'd been at the hostel, and he approached Mrs. Ryan with some bills again. She took some of them, and pushed back some change, which he pocketed. A thick haze had settled over everything, and Paul sensed October closing in on November: dank winter overcomes the Emerald Isle. Now he woke shivering in the night. The comforter provided by the Seagull was insufficient against the chill of the unheated room. David began to have nightmares. Sometimes he would cry out in his sleep and thrash about. He still went out some evenings, always asking Paul to go along, but Paul had the feeling David wasn't going to the pub at all. He saw him in town on a trip he made in himself, to purchase some supplies. David walked across the square with his overcoat flapping down around his ankles, and Paul called out to him, but David either didn't hear or ignored him.

It was only the four of them left there: he and David, and Rosie, and the American girl. He'd not noticed when the girls from Cork went away but he had not seen them in a very long time. It no longer seemed curious to him that they rarely interacted, moving through the days as though each had erected an invisible but impenetrable barrier against the others.

One day Paul found himself sitting on his bunk composing a letter to his sister. He broke down crying. He wanted to go home. He paced up and down the room, cursing this grey inhospitable place, these people who flitted like ghosts here. He felt frantic to phone the airlines, to go screaming cross the Atlantic and home again. He became panicked. Some nights before he'd dreamed of a mushroom cloud, and he wept, imagining this the last place left in all the world, and them the only people. He finished his letter to Robin, assuring her he'd be home soon, he just needed to make arrangements. "As a matter of fact," he concluded optimistically, "you'll probably already have heard from me by phone by the time you get this!"

The words would be a talisman. He gave the letter to Mrs. Ryan for posting. Afterwards he thought better of it, but when he asked her about it she stared at him with stolid incomprehension and said, "Postman took it." She still wore that scarf twisted defiantly about her neck, and Paul realized he no longer needed to look at any sort of label on it to confirm that it belonged to Alyssa. And he'd lost so much time here there was no hope of ever catching up to her.

"I'm heading back soon," he told David, who did his exercises faithfully this morning as every morning. David lifted his head to look at him, red-faced.

"You'll be leaving, then?"

"Looks that way," Paul said. "Gotta get back to school. See my family again. My sister was pregnant last I heard. Probably I'm an uncle now." It felt funny to say it.

He walked into town and checked the bus schedules. Several left each day and he could easily connect to one that was Dublin-bound. The lazy appeal of hitchhiking had vanished. He thanked Mrs. Ryan for her hospitality and informed her he'd be leaving early the next morning.

The wind and the sea woke him in the night, just as they had the first night he spent here.

This night, however, was moonless; no figures on the water to frighten him, no restless breathing in the room about him. But the sea was louder than ever before, the crashing of its waves palpably close, as though he could reach out through the window and dip his hand in those cold waters.

Paul woke again at dawn, before the others, and slipped outside.

He'd smoked his last cigarette the night before, and so he stood staring out at the water, nothing to do but gaze at the beam of light.

He climbed up the cliffs, as the German girl and her boyfriend had done, and scrambled down the slick path to the shore.

He found the dinghy waiting there for him. A solid, wooden vessel, splintery planks for seats. At one time he wouldn't have trusted it to take him across a pond.

But this was different.

Paul zipped his coat tighter against the winds, which blew in across the water, and pulled on gloves. Rowing was difficult when the cold numbed your hands, though he wasn't really sure how much rowing he would have to do.

He pushed the boat most of the way into the water. He tried to climb in, still standing on dry land, but the boat tipped sideways and threatened to spill him into the sea as soon as he transferred all his weight. He would have to wade in, up to his shins. He gasped as the icy waters lapped at his jeans and seeped through to his skin.

Paul couldn't remember having handled a boat at all before. After a couple of false starts, in which he merely bobbed on the water and went in circles, he got the hang of it. Strong, slow, steady strokes sent him gliding against the current, against the constant breaking of the waves in towards land.

In the distance, he could see it, the beam of light, guiding his way. A chilling gust blew across him. Inside the jacket he was sweating, but his face, his lips and nose and ears, had gone numb in the cold.

Travelling, he'd always tried to remain on the move.

Paul kept rowing. The wind stung his eyes and extracted tears. Soon, his destination would become clear. The mist closed behind him and the land slipped away, and the glow beckoned him onward in the grey winter morn.

Islander

Donald Murphy

Don't talk down to me, bub, 'cause I don't take that from no man. And let me tell you something else: I've had a bellyful of your kind, comin' out here with your video cameras and your screamin' brats, gettin' good honest folk to pose for your damn home movies - "oh, ain't they cute! with them red bandannas and them funny shoes. Hold that pitchfork up a little higher, will ya, sport?" - yeah, you heard me right, lookin' down your noses at good people you ain't fit to be mentioned in the same breath as, people that know what work is, that know the hind end of a donkey from the front, which is more than I can say for you and your pack of pasty, camera-snappin', know-it-all...

Wait a minute! Where do you think you're goin'? Come back here and finish your drink! Hell, you're a touchy one, ain't you? I didn't mean nothin' personal. That's better. Sit down. Get a hold of yourself, for Christ's sake! Oh, I know I get riled up, but let me explain a few things so you understand good and clear. This island has been ruined, *ruined* - sold off piece by piece, all because some travel agent writes up a brochure that says: "here the old customs live on forever; untouched by time" - hell, I read it myself - "a livin' museum of tradition", one of 'em said. Well, you just look around and tell me if you see any of these "untouched customs." Because they're gone, every last one of 'em. And it makes me so damn mad that sometimes I'm just ready to bust.

Now, I got nothin' against mainlanders - my own granddaddy was one, they tell me. Came out here and married my Old Gram when she wasn't but twelve years old, then got himself drowned in a squall off Drunkard's Point. Old Gram kept a wick burnin' in a jar of seal fat and put it in the window every night, hopin' he'd see it and come home. But he never did and Old Gram worked the fields herself till the day she died. She was brown and wrinkled as an old leather purse and had a swing on her'd knock your teeth loose and send you flyin' clean into next week. It was her raised me up, after my own daddy drowned and my ma got trampled by a team of ponies.

Anyways, you wouldn't have recognized this place back then. Sure, it was a hard life, but we had everything we needed and we didn't need nothin' from the outside. All this jabber about tradition! In those days, we knew what was right and what was wrong. You mainlanders think we're all simple but, I'll tell you, to live out here a man had to fight, and back then there wasn't no question what you was fightin' against. Maybe you ain't followin' me. Why don't you have another one and I'll tell you a story I ain't told nobody in fifty years or more. You listen hard and maybe you'll learn somethin' about what makes the Devil run when an honest man looks him straight in the eye.

I couldn't have been more than ten at the time. Oh, I was a wild one, but no different than any other boy my age. I went to church every Sunday, to school when I had to, and crab fishin' whenever I got the chance. And I tried to do everything my old Gram told me, because I knew what I'd have waitin' for me at home if I didn't.

Well, one night she sent me out to the strand to gather snails, like I'd done a hundred times before. It was warm and there was a big moon so I was takin' my time, walkin' and dreamin', I guess, out there amongst the kelp and the driftwood. I used to love them summer evenin's when it seemed like all the creatures of the night was comin' out to keep you company - crickets chirpin', bats swoopin' down from the hills. A stripey owl'd fly past once in a while and there was silver geckos all over the rocks, runnin' two by two like they always do and sparklin' in the moonlight.

My snail bucket was only half full but I was enjoyin' myself so much that I decided to sit for a while by that pointy rock you probably seen out there - the Siren's Steeple, we call it. I don't figure much of anything was goin' on in my head by this time. I was just listenin' to the surf and starin' out across the strand, all white under the moon, when I saw the queerest damn thing. I sat up to get a better look and all of a sudden the hair was standin' up at the back of my neck. Because out there, walkin' across the sand, side by side and just far enough away so I couldn't see 'em too clear, was three black shapes. And, boy, they was like nothin' I'd ever seen before.

The one in the middle was tall, thirty hands high must have been; tall and thin and walked like he had a mainmast for a backbone. Seemed like only his feet was movin'. The rest of him was steady and straight as an old ash tree.

The one on the left was a head shorter and where the middle one was straight as a pole, this one was all curves and swishy movements, like an eel when you corner one at low tide. From the way it swished and swayed, I thought it had to be a woman. Sounds crazy but I could've sworn she was floatin' and her feet wasn't even touchin' the ground.

The third one, the one on the right, was the queerest of all. It was a tiny thing, no higher than the waist of the tall one and round and stubby, except for the legs – they was long and spindly, like a whoopin' crane's. One was shorter than the other and this little creature was hobblin' along, dippin' this way and that and tryin' to keep up with the other two. It was a horrible thing to see; I seen a dwarf once in a circus and it wasn't no stranger than this little feller.

The three of 'em was walkin' calm as you please across the beach in the direction of Skull Hill, while I stood there with my mouth hangin' open and rubbin' my eyes and, well, wonderin'... You see, I knew everyone on the island – hell, there weren't many of us in those days, and there sure wasn't anyone like these three. And back then we didn't get tourists. Hadn't even been a boat from Port Stark for three weeks or more. Wasn't no strangers around or I would've known it for sure. We're not folk for keepin' secrets and hidin' things from our neighbors like you mainlanders.

Anyway, I started deducin' and speculatin' and the only thing I came up with was that I was lookin' at three spooks, from Hell probably, and up to no damn good, that was for sure. I'd heard about spooks and ghosts and demons, of course, ever since I can remember. They was everywhere in them days – I guess they still are but camouflaged so the tourists won't recognize 'em. But back then, this island was crawlin' with 'em. Everybody knew it and did what they could to protect theirselves, not get too close to a lynchin' tree, for instance, and make sure their front doors was painted blue. I'd never seen no spirits up close before but I had a good, strong fear of 'em just like everybody else. And now there was three live ones not 100 yards away and me just a scrawny little fry not out of short pants yet.

Well, I got so scared that I dropped my snail bucket and turned around and ran all the way home like a scalded hare. I stayed the rest of the night buried down under the covers, sayin' the "Please Father" and tryin' to keep my teeth from chatterin'. Oh, I had some awful thoughts about what I'd just seen! But when the sun was just comin' up and I'd calmed down a bit, I started thinkin' about somethin' else. Old Gram'd be wantin' her breakfast and I hadn't brought back even one snail. Not only that, but I'd left her best tin bucket lyin' out there on the strand. She wasn't goin' to be too happy about that and my backside still smarted from the last hidin' she give me. To make a long story short, nothin's as scary in the daytime as it is in the dead of night and so by the time the sun was all the way up I decided to go fetch the bucket and save myself a whippin'.

It was a fine mornin', I remember. The sea was glassy and you could see the peak of Old Baldy way out there across the channel. Sure enough, the bucket was right where I left it and there was nothin' strange or un-usual anywhere that I could see; it was a normal day just like any other. Well, I hurried and gathered up what snails I could find; I was goin' to get my ears boxed for bringin' home so few, but it was better than nothin'.

I should've gone straight home for breakfast but I always was a curi-ous one. I couldn't help takin' a little walk across the beach where I'd seen them three... Truth is, I was startin' to doubt I'd seen anything at all! Maybe it'd only been a dream – I was thinkin' that was what Old Gram'd say if I told her. But then I looked down and I saw 'em. No doubt about it, it was the tracks of them creatures right there in the sand.

This is goin' to be hard for you to believe but I swear it on my mama's gold teeth. Well, there was three sets of tracks right enough, but they was-n't normal footprints, like a human bein' would make. Every four or five yards, they changed. For a while I'd see what looked like the tracks of a chicken, then the hoofprints of a goat, then the paws of a bear, then they was of a dog, a pig, a big old gander, a lizard hoppin' on its hind legs; there was even a long slithery trail like a snake would make. Three sets of prints, you understand, but not one of a human foot! Damnedest thing I ever seen! Finally, they disappeared into a big field of dogweed – the one right at the foot of Skull Hill – and I wasn't about to follow 'em any further.

Well, on my way home, I made up my mind to tell Old Gram the truth. This was somethin' real serious and I was only a little boy. Whether anybody believed me or not, I had to tell what I saw.

She was waitin' for me in the kitchen and sure she was about to tan my hide when I stopped her and made her listen to the whole story. Her face was set like a gopher trap that's ready to spring but I thought I saw somethin' steal into those grey eyes of hers, a kind of a worried look, that I took to mean she believed at least some of what I was sayin'. But when I finished, she grabbed away the bucket and dragged me outside by the collar. Told me to clean out the henhouse and then wash down her old sow 'cause she was fixin' to sell it. And I wasn't gettin' no breakfast till I did. Maybe a little honest work would clear some of the pipe-dreams and laziness out of my thick head, she said.

Well, it just about did and by lunchtime I was so hungry, tired, and dirty that I wasn't thinkin' about them spooks no more. And I made sure I kept my mouth shut around Old Gram. Every once in a while I'd see her crossin' the yard to do her own chores or peepin' out the window from behind her lace curtain and it seemed like she was eyein' me a little funny. It was always hard to read that woman's face but I could've sworn somethin' was eatin' her about what I'd said. When I was knee-deep in pig-slop and almost finished with the sow, she finally came out, real sol-emn-like, and told me to get washed up and have somethin' to eat. Then, after I'd chowed down, she handed me a pot of buttered eels and told me to take it over to Dr. Borka. And she said while I was there to tell him just what I'd told her.

Now, I was only a kid, but to talk to Dr. Borka about somethin', especially somethin' like this, made me feel like I was pretty damn important. And to send me over there, Old Gram must've thought it was serious business, too. You see, a problem for Dr. Borka was a problem that nobody could figure out or was too scared to handle theirselves.

These days, you won't find a man like him on this island nor any other. When he died, we all said we'd never see the like of him again, and we was right. Because he was a combination of all them things that now you only read about or remember – brains, common sense, book-learnin', righteousness... He didn't stand for no nonsense in any shape or form and just havin' him here made us feel protected, like we was all in good hands.

Sure, we was afraid of him, too. If you had any evil in your heart, or any sins to hide – and, hell, who doesn't? – you felt lower than a hedge slug when you talked to him. He was the most upright, moral man I ever knew and he'd put the fear of God into anyone who wasn't on the straight-and-narrow. Oh, I wasn't dumb; I knew Old Gram was hopin' he'd know what to do about whatever was out there on the strand.

Now, Dr. Borka would help folks whenever they needed it, but he wasn't what you'd call social. He lived all by himself in a little house on the edge of town and spent most of his time readin' and studyin' and speculatin' about things the rest of us never even heard of. When I knocked on his door that morning, I heard him say come in, but it was like he wasn't really payin' attention, like he was buried in his books as usual.

That was what you remembered most about his house. Books everywhere – tall stacks of 'em leanin' this way and that and covered with dust. That, and the glass cases full of butterflies, bugs and beetles he had hangin' all over his walls. He was an expert on 'em, just like he was on plants, rocks, herbs, seaweed... It was scary all the things that man knew! But he was a Doctor of Divinity and it was spiritual things people usually asked him for advice about.

Well, I weaved through that dark, dingy livin' room of his and went back into his study. He was sittin' there at his big oak desk, just the top of his grey head and them cold blue eyes showin' above the books piled up in front of him. I saw him look up at me and I knew he was waitin' to hear what I had on my mind. So I went round to the side of his desk and set down the pot of eels and then, after I took a deep breath, I just spewed out the whole thing – spooks, snails, sow and all.

He listened without askin' me nothin', and all the while them eyes had me fixed like one of his butterflies; they burned right into me, lookin' me up and down, evaluatin' everything I said, but at the same time makin' me feel like I'd done the right thing by comin' to him. And then, when there wasn't no more to tell, he stood up and went over to the window. He was a giant of a man, with shoulders like an ox and big, powerful hands. Seemed like his head almost touched the ceiling. Well, he looked out the window for a while, then he came over and knelt down so he he could look me right in the eye. I was scared, but at the same time I felt safe that I was on the same side as him. I say the same side because I knew somehow we was in for a fight.

Then he started talkin', in a real calm voice, explainin' things to me, and I could tell he didn't think it was no pipe-dream. The world was full of powers, he said, some of 'em good and some real bad and just like we got born to be good, others came into the world just to be evil and to make trouble for the good folks. What I'd seen wasn't the half of it, because Dr. Borka had been observin' things lately and one after another all pointed to a catastrophe that was brewin' on the island and that only we as realized it could prevent.

He told me a few of these things. Liddy Goodge's cow had gone dry, just like that, and now so had Boo Spinkley's. Sap Starling, the light-house keeper, was still in bed with a bellyache that nobody could explain and his wife swore that somethin' had swooshed down the chimney one mornin' and gone into the soup she was makin'. More things, too; out in the marsh all the toads was dyin' and nobody knew why, and now a two-headed goat'd been born over in North Town. And he, Dr. Borka, had been watchin' the clouds and seen things in 'em – I don't know what, but he could read what they said and he knew we had to act fast. Finally, he put his big heavy hand on my shoulder and said to me, "Boy, are you interested in saving this island?" Of course, I said I was and I asked him how. He thought for a second and then he told me to meet him that night at midnight on the old beach road and not to tell nobody about it. He said he had somethin' mighty important to do and he needed me to help.

I can't say his words calmed me down any. I didn't know nothin' about fightin' ghosts or whatever they was and I tried as hard as I could not to think back to the night before. But I'll be damned if I wasn't excited about the whole thing at the same time, like it was one hell of an adventure we was settin' out on, and with somebody like Dr. Borka along I figured I'd be as safe as anyone could be. Anyway, he sent me home with a note to give to Old Gram and when she read it, she didn't say nothin' more that night – didn't make me do no more chores, neither. We just sat there the two of us and waited, nervous as a couple of wharf cats, until it was time for me to go. And then, just before the clock struck twelve, she shooed me out the door and off I went down that lonely road that leads to the strand.

Well, it was eerie out there, that's all I can say. The surf was poundin' like it always does but aside from that it seemed so quiet that whatever sounds I was hearin', whether it was the call of a razorbill or the hoot of a barn-squatter, seemed like they was all wrapped up in a big, thick blanket of night. I could see where I was goin' 'cause of the moon but them shadows along the side of the road seemed like they was watchin' me, and who knows?, maybe they was. Then, all of sudden, I saw a big, dark shape in the road, like a bear standin' on its hind legs, and I stopped dead, my heart pumpin' like an old steam drill.

A second later, I heard someone callin' my name and I knew it was only Dr. Borka waitin' for me like he was supposed to be. When I got up to where he was standin', he didn't say nothin', just turned and motioned for me to follow him. He had a big sack over his shoulder and he gave it to me to carry. It was heavy and things was clankin' around inside. And he had a long metal bar in one hand, like a walkin' stick but with a little U-shaped piece at one end of it. I was about to ask him what it was for but he gave me a sign to hush up and then it was all I could do to keep up with his long, swift strides.

Well, we came up over that ridge of sand that lies in back of the beach and went down to the spot where I'd been snail-gatherin'. The Steeple was juttin' up like a knife stuck into the moon and we stopped for a minute right under it. I pointed out to where I'd seen them creatures and Dr. Borka just nodded his head, like it wasn't no surprise. Then we took off walkin' again, across the strand and straight for that field where I'd seen 'em disappear.

Bein' out there on the beach gave me a real bad feelin'. There was a mist hangin' over the water's edge and behind it the ocean was roarin' like a thousand voices all together. It was bigger'n anything on earth, I thought; it could swallow you, swallow the whole island just like that, and we'd all be down in its black belly. I started prayin' to myself – "God bless Old Gram and Aunt Viny and Mr. Bloodletter and all the kids at school, and please, please, please save us all from them spooks..."

I don't know if Dr. Borka saw anything creepin' through that cold fog or slitherin' out there across the beach, but if he did, it didn't bother him none. Damned if we didn't plow right into the dogweed and keep marchin' straight ahead till we came to the other end of it and that pile of rocks – Hell's Ladder, we call it – that makes kind of a natural staircase up the side of Skull Hill. It was a place I wouldn't never've gone on my own, much less in the dead of night, but Dr. Borka wasn't scared of nothin' and I didn't reckon I could turn back now.

Now, up on Skull Hill there lived an old witch by the name of Enny Ocker. The islanders'd driven her out of town, oh, way before I was born, and she lived up there all by herself, half-crazy and deaf as a post, in an old shack she'd built out of driftwood and washed-up boards. I used to see her sometimes scrabbling for mussels down at the far end of the strand and me and my buddies'd throw rocks at her to keep her away. Old Gram used to say she could paralyze you just by lookin' at you, make your poker shrivel up and your charlies drop off before you even knew it. They said that wherever she pissed nothin' would ever grow again, and it must've been true, 'cause the whole top of Skull Hill was just as barren as it could be; I don't know what she lived on - seaweed, mussels, and snails, I expect. What she liked most was little boys, boiled in their own fat, said Old Gram, and you can bet I kept my distance from her. Oh, she was a horrible, vicious thing but you didn't see her hardly ever. If she'd come into town, people would've taken care of her good and quick.

Now, it was pretty clear, under that big shiny moon, that we was headin' straight for old Enny's shack. It was a pitiful, ramshackle thing, nailed together with no rhyme nor reason, full of gaps and holes where the boards didn't fit together right - must've been frightful cold up there in the winter. I'd never seen it close up before and it looked like now we was sneakin' right up to the front door, real slow and cautious, and Dr. Borka was givin' the place a once-over with his old eagle-eye.

So all them strange happenin's got somethin' to do with Enny Ocker, I thought. I never would've guessed it. But Dr. Borka knew a hell of lot more than a little snip like me. I tell you that man could sniff out evil like a bloodhound after a stoat.

We tippy-toed up to the door and he put his ear to one of the cracks. He made a sign for me to do the same and, even with the surf poundin' out there in the night, I could hear somebody snorin' inside. And somethin' smelled bad in there, just like you'd expect evil to smell. We was quiet as two possums, even though we knew the old woman couldn't hear. You never can tell - she probably had other powers we didn't know about. You couldn't never trust a witch.

Well, the first thing Dr. Borka did was to take that metal walkin' stick of his and slide the U-shaped piece on it under the knob of Enny's front door. Then he fixed the other end of it into the ground and propped a big rock behind it so that nobody could open the door from inside. Old Enny was trapped like a mink in a barrel.

Then he opened the sack and started takin' things out of it. There was a long, rolled-up rubber hose, then a big tin funnel, and finally a metal cannister, like we get molasses in, with a screw-on cap and a wire handle. My eyes was wide like saucers watchin' all of this, him gettin' his witch-fightin' equipment all organized and inspectin' the outside of the shack, peepin' through the cracks, and sortin' it all out in his head.

Didn't take him long. First, he unrolled the hose and put one end of it through a crack that was about knee-level next to the door. Then, real slow, he slid it inside. He kept pushin' until he was holdin' only about three or four feet of it in his hand. Then he stuck the funnel onto the end he was holdin' and handed it to me. He made me lift it over my head so that the hose hung straight down and then went off into the shack. And while I was doin' this, he unscrewed the cap from the cannister.

Whatever was inside had a powerful smell – even stronger than what Old Gram used to take for her rheumatism. Anyway, while I held up the funnel, Dr. Borka poured all of the liquid down it. After a while, I saw some of it seepin' out from under the door in a long, shiny puddle. I was scared that Enny was goin' to wake up, but it seemed like she was only snorin' louder.

When the cannister was empty, he screwed the cap back on, then pulled out the hose and rolled it up again. And then I held the sack open while he put everything back into it. Nothin' had happened yet and the night, except for the surf and the owls and the bats, was as hushed as it could be. But I felt a whole lot calmer for some reason and I remember thinkin' that there was one thing that wasn't never goin' to change, and that was this island that I was born on and that was always goin' to belong to me and my kin. I felt it there rock-solid under my feet and I wasn't fearin' the ocean no more because this big old block of stone was even stronger than all them rollin', poundin' waves.

Dr. Borka put his hand on my shoulder and led me off a little distance away, and we stood there in the moonlight lookin' at that poor, dilapidated pile of timber. Then he whispered to me to stay put and he walked, calm as a boiled clam, back up to the door. I saw him make a kind of a sign with one hand, some priesty stuff it looked like. Then he took out a box of matches, lit one, and then turned it in his hand so it blazed up in a real good flame. That little old match seemed like a lantern shinin' out there in the dark. Finally, with them same nerves of steel and that same cool-headed know-how, he tossed the lit match into the puddle of liquid.

Well, I never seen nothin' like that before nor after, not even on Island Day and only once or twice at the picture show. That shack, that was all rotten boards and dried-up tree branches, just exploded from inside in a great big ball of yellow flames. They was shootin' out through the cracks in the walls and in the roof and there was a blast of burnin' wind that I could feel on my face like a solid wall of heat. And all of a sudden it was like daylight out there! There wasn't no more creepin' shadows, nothin' that could lurk nor hide in the light of that roarin', blazin' bonfire.

And standin' there with his arms in the air and his face all lit up by the flames was that lion of a man who'd risked his own neck to save us all, and now he looked like a real giant, wavin' his fists and shoutin' up into the heavens.

"Begone!" I heard him shout. "Back into Hell with you demons, back to your dark, dirty dungeons, away from the light and the countenance of God, and back to your eternal punishment!"

He must've known how scared I was 'cause he knelt down and put his arm around me. Then he pointed his giant's finger up at the clouds of brown smoke that was formin' in the air and said to me:

"Fear nothing, my boy! Behold on the wings of smoke the damned and wretched, the evil ones who would destroy us all. Behold them now as they flee the wrath of God. Behold them as they writhe in helpless agony! Hear their cries of defeat!"

And I looked up at that towerin' cloud and I squinted my eyes and, yes, I saw 'em, hundreds of 'em, twistin' and squirmin' in the smoke, and then I listened hard and I heard 'em, too. I heard 'em screamin', heard 'em screamin' out over the sound of the surf and the cracklin' of the flames, screamin' somethin' terrible, but it wasn't no use because Dr. Borka had whipped 'em once and for all and them awful spooks wasn't goin' to be botherin' us never again.

All right, you've had your entertainment, so pay up and get the hell out of here. You can go back and tell it to every damn mainlander you know, for all I care. Makes no difference to me what you all think. You just tell 'em you heard it from a man who remembers what things used to be like, and wouldn't trade places with them for all the oysters in Shagley Bay.

Go on now. I got better things to do than sit here jawin' with you all night.

Storysville

Alison Davies

Elias should have been happy. Things had turned out unexpectedly good for the sour mannered man with the bursting gut and an equally throbbing rage. He could have been trussed up like a turkey, dangling by the scrawny flap of skin that splayed limply beneath his chin. He could have been squirming for that last parcel of air that would sustain him till the final pulse of life dissolved to spit on the ground.

Instead he was waking on strawberry striped sheets with the clean glint of sunlight speckling the ceiling and a cool jug of water to wash in. The room, though essentially bare, had a welcoming feel after hours of saddle sore marching through unrelenting landscapes. In fact it would be true to say Elias would certainly be dancing with delight on those old callused toes if he could remember how he got there. He couldn't blame this blank period of memory lapse on the savageries of drink, not this time. He'd been dry for two days, cursing and hissing at the unfairness of the law with nothing to sweeten the painful cards he'd been dealt.

He lifted himself nervously off the bed. His head felt thick and sore, prickled by a thousand steaming needles. His eyes watered with irritation, salty rivulets tickled his nose, melting into the sallow leather of his cheeks. Something was not right. Moving to the window he surveyed the street below. A curve of dust path bordered by wooden buildings, and a saloon across the way. The jaded pattern of paint licked the windows and the sign creaked lazily 'The Last Shot'. 'Sure is a strange name for a watering hole' thought Elias to himself. He watched for signs of life; an old man slept fitfully on the step his cranky head lolled forward, but it didn't seem to bother him. A tall angular woman bustled along the sidewalk her skirts clearing a path. Her face appeared grim and full of concern. She didn't look up or speak. 'Well they be a right cheery bunch in this place.' Elias concluded before turning to the washbowl.

When Elias Duke finally made it down the swirl of stairs to the hotel lobby the full brightness of the sun had hijacked the skies, covering everything with an unnatural golden haze. Dust swam through the air seizing Elias by the throat and he spluttered awkwardly.

"S'cuse me Sir." He drawled. "Know this sounds a little stupid, but can you tell me where I am?"

The small ferret-eyed man tweaked his glasses, staring at Elias incredulously.

"Your right there, it does sound damn foolish."

Elias hovered for moment, trying to decide in his mind whether to grab the insufferable jerk by the throat or take a breath and ask again.

"You're in Storysville." He replied eventually.

"Storysville?"

"S'what I said, isn't it? What's the matter with you? Got cloth ears?"

Elias froze, anger pulsing through his veins.

"I ain't ever heard of it before." He snapped.

The man stroked his shiny head and then smiled falsely.

"Well now, I guess cos you ain't heard of it, then it don't exist." He twanged.

Elias slammed his hand down on the smooth dark wood of the desk.

"Are you being funny with me, cos I wouldn't do that if I was you. Finer men have paid the price."

The man sniggered, unconcerned by the sudden outburst.

"You don't seem to have grasped the concept yet, do you?" He smiled. "There ain't nothing you can do to me that hasn't been tried before. I'm just the innkeeper shall we say. All's I do is find you a place to lay your head, and serve your liqueur." He shuffled out from under the desk and busied himself clearing glasses. "If you've got a problem, you've got a problem. But keep me out of it."

Elias stared in wonder. His feeling of unease had returned. Where the hell was this honky tonk town?

"Look," he said trying to appease his fury. "I just want to know where I am, who runs this place and where I can get me a horse so's that I can leave."

The hotelier regarded him with a feigned amusement, his slitty eyes squeezed even tighter together.

"You can't leave here. Nobody leaves Storysville. Didn't I say?"

Elias sat crookedly on the step, tracing rainbow patterns in the dust with a knobby finger. His collar pulled high to disguise the tawny flesh of his neck. His old skin jacket had seen better days. Any other time Elias would have socked the fella with the prissy attitude right on the end of his puckered nose, but this wasn't any other time. His intuition flared with the ashes of fear and ignorance. He didn't understand what was going on and that scared him more than anything. Weasel features had explained that Storysville didn't exist, not outside the limits of the real world, his world. He said it was a lost town where people sort of drifted. There was no escape, just a life of emptiness with other like-minded souls.

He stabbed a finger into the powdery earth. Sure felt real enough to him and yet something in his tainted heart almost believed old weasel features. Something uncompromising stirred in those unholy recesses. Elias sat, so deep in his own contemplation that he failed to notice the midnight clothed stranger with the flapping black poncho watching him. The apparition moved closer, huge folds of ebony blowing mysteriously on an unseen breeze. His dark brimmed hat shielded most of his features, but when Elias looked up he caught a very faint glimpse of death. He squinted, blinded by the charred mess that lurked in the shadows.

"Who in the hell are you?" He reeled. "Jees... you gave me a fright."

The figure stood - bemused or afraid, Elias could not tell.

"I am a story, just like you, just like everyone in this foul place." He hissed seductively.

Elias groaned. More riddles to confuse him. Why couldn't anybody talk straight in this town?

"What do you mean story? How can YOU be a story?" He sneered grating his toe along the gravel.

The figure bent down close, his sheathed face inches away, and when he spoke Elias could smell bones on his breath. Crumbling yellow bones.

"We are the stories they'll be telling forever. We are the decrepit, and the despised. The ones who dared to leave a trail of sorrow behind them....for this, they keep us alive in their minds. Living here in a town that doesn't exist, face to face with our crimes."

"I don't understand." Elias murmured, as cranky fingertips prodded his spine.

Yellow Bones smiled. Elias could feel mushy folds of skin crack and contort.

"My name used to be Luke Ridgley. I murdered my family. I slaughtered my brother, my father, and finally my poor dear mother. Split them apart. Ripped them open and then set them alight." He sniggered and the sound fell unnaturally to the ground.

"My god," Elias whispered. "I do remember the stories about you. They said you had the devil in you, they said you tore those folks up pretty bad...but that was, well it must have been at least 50 years ago!"

Yellow Bones chuckled, "'I got burned too, real bad. But it was worth it, oh yes. See all I was left with was scars. But they're gone!" He threw back his head, his hat tumbling to the floor to reveal a tapestry of severed flesh, all lumpy and distorted. Ice blue eyes stared wildly from seeping wounds. Elias screamed, staggering from his perch on the step. Running down the street, running faster than his tired limbs could take him. Hurtling for the 'The Last Shot' saloon. God knows he needed a drink; he needed something to stop the sickness gurgling inside. The sound of crooked laughter followed him as he burst through the saloon doors. Would the diseased spectre come after him? Would he dare to follow in here? Elias glanced around furtively, looking for signs of human life. Inside in the fusty darkness was the woman from earlier. She sat staring at the table. Her pinched features deep in reflection.

"S'cuse me mam," spluttered Elias, sweat pouring from the tip of his nose.

"There's... there's, some kind of burnt up.... I dunno, some kind of loon out there!" He yelled looking round the room. The words dissolved into dirt. The bar was virtually dead but for the haggard woman and the waiflike bartender and neither of them seemed to take in what he had said.

"Didn't your hear me?" He shrieked in panic, "What's wrong with you people? There's some kind of monster out there! He's trying to get me!"

The woman tapped her fingers patiently on the table, scraping her nails feverishly along the wood.

"Yellow Bones." She rasped. "It's only Yellow Bones."

Elias leaned an arm against the bar trying desperately to catch his breath.

"He.... he's a murderer. He told me."

This time she raised her pointy jaw and looked deep into his eyes. Her face had a reptilian quality, and her tongue flashed noisily between her teeth as she spoke.

"So are you. Murdered that young woman, strangled her with your own bare hands and then when she was dying tore at her flesh like an animal." She slavered. "Don't worry dear Elias, your secret's safe with us. We all have our own stories here."

Elias gripped the side of the bar tighter, splintered wood piercing his hand. The tiny prickles of pain served as a reminder that he wasn't actually stuck in some nightmare. This was reality. This was cruel.

"I killed my husband, only difference is I did it over time. He died a lingering death, years of punishment. I drove him to it."

Elias swayed softly. What had he gotten himself into? Was this some sort of town for decaying freaks - or had he really stepped into another world?

"No, no I don't want to hear anymore...please. I need to get out of here!" Elias whimpered, his legs buckled weakly.

"You'll never get out of here. You'll never leave. You can't." She whispered smugly.

Elias looked from the bartender to the lizard lady and then back to the door. If he could bolt now, if he could manage to move his jelly legs, get out the door and past that fried up abomination, perhaps he stood a chance. He needed a horse, but there were no horses here. Did it matter? He thought, perhaps he could just run, carried forward by the horror that burned inside him. Taking a huge gulp of air he lurched carelessly for the doors his whole body weight exploding into the afternoon heat.

"Hey Buddy, I knew you'd return! Want to hear some more?" Yellow Bones swaggered towards him, loose skin dangling in mid air. Elias wailed. His feet shuffled beneath in a desperate struggle with gravity.

"Do you want to know how they screamed when I cut off their ears? They sounded like mad coyotes." He continued edging ever closer.

"NO!" Screamed Elias. "NO Please NO!" His ankle twisted and in a confusion of limbs he sprawled to the ground.

"...and you should have seen the blood", Yellow Bones sneered. "It was sooooooo thick and beautiful!"

"NO." Elias convulsed.

The air shifted. For a moment the world went black.

Elias could only feel a searing pain darting through his temples, a deep incongruous sensation. Then in a rush of madness, lightness drowned him and everything was different.

Storysville was gone, its bleak landscape shattered, and instead a sea of expectant faces gazed up at him. A mass of disgusted, bitter expressions. Townsfolk, people he knew, all regarding him with that same hateful gaze. He was about to ask them what was wrong, about to ask why they were gathered before him, staring intently when he felt the chafing bite around his neck. He saw the glint of dusk behind the clouds. He saw the doom-ridden skies above him and felt the rope garrotting his windpipe. He knew where he was, and he knew with a refreshed torment his fate. The pain came fast, the sharp vibrating crack of hollow bones and then Elias faded. The town watched, gleaning some sort of satisfaction that justice had prevailed, and a worthless life destroyed. And of course the simple act of hanging should have been the end of it. No more Elias Duke. But, as so often happens in these situations a wretched memory is allowed to live on. Trapped in the minds of those who refuse to forget.

Somewhere in the heart of Storysville one man's embittered cries could be heard - a sordid tale of life which continues through eternity.

The Graven

Simon Bestwick

Danny and Karen walked along the Scarborough seafront hand in hand. The sun danced on the blue sea.

It was a bright, warmish Easter, and in the week they'd been there, they'd partaken of all the pleasures on offer- including the dubious ones of the local fish and chips. Scarborough supposedly had at least one of the finest chippies in the country, but if that was so, they had yet to encounter it.

There were the big arcades that lit up the sea fronts at night. There were second hand bookshops to browse in, for they both loved to read. And the National Student Drama Festival was on. They'd been to see half a dozen shows of varying quality, and Karen had made Danny laugh with some of her tales of her time up here in her college days.

But it had palled. There was only so much you could do, so many walks you could take or books read before you wanted something new. Danny thought he might have found it.

"There's a little village up the coast, or what's left of it. Place called Newcross. Supposed to be worth seeing. Want to go?"

Karen smiled sleepily in the bright warm sunshine. "Why not?"

Newcross wasn't much of a village. It was comparatively new, built in the nineteen twenties, unusual for fishing villages in this part of the world. The reason for that lay about half a mile due south of the village, to the remains of the old village of Knightscross.

A narrow winding road took them down to Knight's Bay, the little inlet that served as the village's harbour. They wandered down the quiet, pretty beach of rough shingle, following a rusty signpost marked OLD KNIGHTSCROSS VILLAGE.

The cliff pushed sharply out in front on them, almost into the water itself. They stepped around. Karen's jaw dropped open. Even Danny, who'd known what they would find, was impressed.

The patch of beach lay between two abrupt protrusions of cliff face. In between lay a jumble of scattered, wave-worn masonry, much of it still recognisable, despite the years' passage. A church-spire, its framework near-denuded of tiling, stuck up out the sand it lay half-buried in at an angle of forty-five degrees.

"What?" Karen was stunned.

"There's more," Danny told her. He led her round the second cliff face. She swore as a wave washed over her foot, realising as they went that this second out sweep was far narrower than the first, only ten feet wide at most. Past it, the coast swept on, the cliff lowering till it merged with the sand and shingle. On this side, too, there was wreckage, and as they walked among the fallen buildings, her foot banged against something. She looked down and saw a skull grinning up at her from the sand, dried seaweed clinging to it like hair. She took a horrified step back. Near it, a smooth-worn cross of grey stone stuck up, leaning to one side, also hung with weed.

"Newcross was built after the storm in 1897," Danny said. "The old village fell straight into the sea. A lot of people didn't get out in time, but the ones that did set up a new village just past Knight's Bay. All that was left was what was on that bit." He pointed up at the narrow wall of cliff face sticking out from the rest, bisecting the scattered ruins on the beach.

Karen looked up at it with awe. "Anything much on it?"

"Some statue. Supposed to be pretty interesting. Come on, race you there!"

His long, serious face flickered with boyish humour, and she ran with him, laughing, over the beach to the path hewn out of the cliff face.

A fence ran round the sheer cliff edge. There were no other sightseers, for both the new village and the site of the old one were out of the way. From the high vantage point, you could see that it looked as if some starving giant had bitten a chunk out of the coastline. Or it would have were it not for that strange narrow spit of cliff face that divided it and gave it the shape of a softly rounded W.

Fencing also ran along the sides of the spit, which, a plaque informed them, was Knight's Point. Most of its hundred foot length was bare but for sparse, wiry grass.

Except for the statue at the end.

They approached it.

No words were on the statue itself, or its plinth, but a well-worn stand beside it, presumably placed by the National Trust or some such, gave what little information was known. The statue was thought to date back to the Middle Ages, although there was no sure proof. The earliest mention of it was in 1664. No one knew who or what it was meant to represent.

Looking at it, it was easy to see how the lost village had gained its name. It represented, quite simply, a knight and a doorway. The door and the knight's attire looked medieval enough. The sculpture was eroded to featurelessness in parts by a century of wind and rain, but in other places, the attention to detail was clear. The grain of the planks in the door. The nails on the knight's left hand, which was pressed against it. The links in the chain mail.

The door seemed to be bulging slightly in its frame as if someone or something was trying to force it wide. The knight's left hand and foot kept it shut, while the sword in his right arm was raised to strike should the door give way.

It was the knight's face that had suffered the most, worn to a near-blank. The nose was a nub, the eyes little more than traces. But there was a thin line of mouth, and above it you could just make out what looked like a bushy moustache.

"What the hell's he keeping out?" wondered Karen.

"Maybe he isn't," Danny murmured. "Maybe he's keeping something in."

She looked at him curiously, but he said nothing more.

There were no souvenir stalls on the cliff, or cafes or suchlike- Newcross needed and valued the little tourist trade that the old village brought their way. So it was there that they went to shop for knickknacks and trinkets, there that they bought a print of an old oil painting of the statue, the head and shoulders, the original dated 1894, just before the sea took the village away. The shopkeeper smiled at Karen with an if-I-was-thirty-years-younger look in his eye; a smile which faded when he looked at Danny. He looked strange then. Afraid? No. The look was almost - *awed.*

He thinks Karen's *that* pretty? Danny thought sardonically, and that was the last he thought of it.

They had coffee and prawn salad in the cafe, and laughed and joked. They wandered the beaches again, inspected the ruins of Knightscross and went on over rolling dunes, making sure to get back before the tide came in. Danny was glad of the exercise, because he'd noticed more than one local glancing their way with looks compounded of trepidation, anxiety and- did he imagine it? - the same awe that he thought he'd glimpsed on the shopkeeper's face.

That's the local yokels for you, he thought, and with that, sought to banish the thoughts from his mind.

A beautiful sunset was falling at the edge of the horizon. They stood and watched it before driving back to Scarborough.

Karen rarely took more than a few minutes to put on all her make up. It was Danny who always spent twenty odd minutes dithering in front of the mirror in the guest house room trying to work out which tie went with which shirt. While she waited, she contemplated the painting. She frowned.

"Dan, come and have a look at this."

He trundled over, a tie in either hand. "Which one?"

She pointed. "That one. Look -"

"You sure?"

"Yes. Shut up and look. The face. It's clearer in this, right?"

"Yeah, course it is. Picture's older, isn't it? The statue was in better shape then."

"That's not what I mean. Look. What's missing?"

Danny frowned, then shrugged. "You tell me."

"The moustache."

Danny squinted at the picture. "Oh, yeah."

The face was a little more clearly defined, the planes of the face squarer than those of the statue they'd seen that day, although that could have been put down to the last hundred years of wear and tear. But there was most definitely no moustache on the statue.

"There was a moustache, wasn't there?"

Danny scratched the two-inch scar that crossed his chin. "I think so. Maybe it was something else?"

"Like what?"

Danny had no answer. He shrugged. "Who cares? Are we going for a Chinese or what?"

She took a last long look at the picture, then she shrugged too. "Yeah, let's go."

That night, Danny had the dream.

It was night. He was standing on Knight's Point, walking towards the statue. There was a storm rising. Thunder rumbled across the sea. Lightning scrabbled on the water and the dry land. A yellow, smoky, glow flickered behind the dark clouds.

The Knight in the statue was straining against the door. There was a loud banging, growing louder and louder, and the door would, every so often, bulge outward startlingly, as if it really was made from planks and not stone. The Knight rocked backwards, then pushed back against the door, and Danny saw that his grey colouring was not stone, but the dull gunmetal sheen of his armour. He was suddenly frightened, and somehow knew that the last thing he wanted to do was to go on. What he should be doing was turning tail and running. But, as is the way of such dreams, his feet carried him on towards the Knight and the doorway.

The Knight turned his head round towards Danny. His face was lined and prematurely old. He looked no older than his mid twenties, despite the thick moustache on his upper lip. His eyes met Danny's. "Help me," he said. His voice was weary and breathless, but still resonant, commanding. "Help me."

Danny woke up.

Karen was curled up against his side, still asleep. A seagull cried, loud, then fading, like an echo of itself.

Danny got up and went to the window. There was a fine view of the sea front, although it was dulled at the moment. The beach was a dull mud colour, and the sea was the dull gunmetal grey of-

-of the Knight's armour. Danny shivered slightly.

The sun was struggling up over the edge of the sea, over a blanket of leaden clouds, like a sleeper rising resentfully from a too-short rest.

Something flickered behind the clouds. Something yellow. Danny tried to tell himself it was just the sun, squirting through a gap in the cloud cover, but he didn't think it was.

Just the dream, he told himself, and went to brew coffee for them both.

The day passed, but it was overcast and chill, without the warmth or cheer of the one before. As they walked listlessly along the beach, Danny found himself glancing over to the cloudbank. Something yellow flickered in it again, beyond denial. Just like in the dream.

And he couldn't be sure, but he thought that when the breeze came in from the sea, he smelled not ozone but sulphur on the wind.

The next morning.

"And you've had the dream for two nights running now? Exactly the same?"

Danny nodded miserably. Karen hugged him. "It'll be OK. Probably just something in the air."

He had a feeling she was more right than she knew.

The dream came again that night, and it was different.

The pounding on the door was louder. It was slowly beginning to puh free of its frame. The Knight's knees were starting to buckle. His gaze, when he turned it onto Danny, was pleading, full of fear, the sight in itself terror-inspiring when cut into the lines of that young-old face, that face that was fully human yet seemed to have been... graven. Yes, that was it, *graven* as if in stone, such was its preternatural strength.

"Help me," gasped the Knight. "You must help. You must help now, or..."

He broke off and turned back to the door, sinews bulging as it cracked open. The yellow light flickered, hot, smoky, gaining strength and substance. A stench of rot and sulphur hit Danny's nostrils like a clutch of knives. A low, decayed chuckle wafted out with it.

And just before the Knight, with a last draining heave, slammed the door shut, Danny caught a glimpse, the merest glimpse, of what was lurking behind that door. It catapulted out of sleep and into a sitting position, a scream clotted in his throat like blood. Karen slept on soundly beside him.

And as he looked, a yellow, smouldering glow crept over the floor through the curtains. He went to the window and looked out.

The storm was building, thunder rumbling in from the night dark sea. Lightning flew. But he knew that the glow that danced behind the storm was something else. Something worse.

It dawned on him as he watched; what was coming and what he would have to do. It all fell into place, the dreams, the strange looks the locals at Newcross had given him, the guttering light and the whiff of sulphur on the sea breeze.

Tears ran down his cheeks as he looked down on Karen, small and still in her sleep. She was no fool, nor was she naive, but now she seemed so young and innocent in her simple trust. So trusting, so sure that she would awake in the morning to find him there, that everything would be as it had been yesterday. When the world was so hostile and deranged, when anything could happen.

A kind of vertigo swept through him. Never till now he had he realised how fragile we all are. How easy it is, how casual, for one act of madness, of violence, of error or unthinking cruelty or sheer blind chance to sweep away all we have and are, in the blinking of the eye. Love and joy. Hope and peace. How vulnerable. How delicate.

How precious.

What he had to do would hurt Karen deeply. He knew that beyond all doubt, but this was for all, for everyone everywhere, and they included Karen. He would harm her out of love.

"Forgive me," he whispered, and risked a touch of his lips to her face as he dressed. She stirred and he stood frozen with fear, no doubt a ludicrous sight with a foot off the ground, his shoe half on and half off.

She sighed and settled back to sleep.

Danny breathed.

Dressed, he went out of the room and the guesthouse on tiptoe. He took the keys to the car, but not the room keys; Karen would need them and he wouldn't. You needed keys to come in, not to go away.

The storm shrieked at its height as he stopped the Honda at Knight's point and got out. The wind drove into him like the flat of a great hand, trying to ward him off. The thunder rolled like the victory dance of some titanic warlord. Perhaps it was.

Danny walked into the wind, the rain driving into him like volleys of spears. The Knight still stood there, straining at the door, lone sentinel against the force beyond, all that held it back from rolling in. Did it seek to colonise the world beyond its own? Or was this its world, one it sought to reclaim, to return to from some unfathomable exile?

He didn't know. Neither did he know what *it* was, nor, were the truth told, did he care to. The brief glimpse he'd caught in his dream had made his heart launch into an impersonation of a heavy metal drummer, and he couldn't even remember what it was he had seen. He suspected his mind may have blanked it out. To see it whole, even for a moment, would strike him dead on the spot.

The fires were burning in the sky. Was a brimstone rain about to fall?

He reached the Knight, who remained as he had been, a silent, unmoving thing of stone. For a moment Danny dared to hope it had all been a dream, imagination, anything but -

- but as he watched, the stone door, impossibly, bulged inwards.

1897. The storm. The force had nearly broken through, then, claiming the town of Knight's Cross, seeking to destroy the material of the barrier that held it in check. Someone had intervened at the last possible moment, making it possible for another century to roll by. A century of wars and suffering and grief, yes, but with all its faults it had not been one devoid of hope. All because this little spit of cliff could still stand against the years, all life, all hope, bound to this place.

All because someone had intervened. All because of one man's sacrifice. And another's before him. And before him. And before him...

And now the duty fell to him.

For Karen, then. No, for all.

Danny stood with his chest against the Knight's back and pressed his hand flat against the door. He pushed his foot against it. His right hand closed around the stone hilt of the stone sword.

And the stone head of the stone man turned towards him.

As he watched, the near-featureless face was sculpted back into being. The faint rims of the eyes deepened, and gained irises and pupils. The mouth grew lips, the moustache broke up into its separate hairs. The nub of nose was stretched out and moulded into shape. The grey stone became pink flesh and blood.

The Knight released the sword into his hand and stepped away, slipping off his iron helmet. "Thank you," he said, gently fitting the helmet onto its new owner. "Good luck."

"You too," Danny said.

The Knight walked away, down the Point that was no longer his.

Danny pushed back against the door as it was shoved towards him, forcing it shut. Something behind it screamed a long, cheated scream.

He smiled and thought of Karen one last time, sleeping safe in her bed, secure as she now had a right to be in the knowledge that the sun would rise.

I love you.

Then he pushed the thoughts of her from his mind and turned back to his task.

Karen woke the next morning to the joyous cries of the gulls. Something of their joy touched her, too, making her smile, until she realised that Danny wasn't there.

As she got out of bed to call for him, the landlady was knocking on her bedroom door, calling her name. She pulled on a dressing gown and answered the summons.

The landlady's face was pale. "The police are here, love. They'd like to speak to you."

She folded Karen in her arms, stricken by the dread and anguish carved suddenly into the girl's face, as if slashed there by a knife.

They found Danny's car abandoned by Knight's Point, the driver's door still ajar. There was no sign of him. Extensive searches up and down the coast found nothing.

Suicide was assumed, but no note was found, although it could have been blown away in the storm. That wracked Karen with the hardest grief, because she would never know now if there was anything she could have done, if she was in some way to blame for this, if the love she'd cherished had died with Danny... or before.

Karen stayed for the rest of the week. By its end, she was ready to go home. The police had released the car to her. Before she left, there was one thing she had to do.

That morning, she drove up to Knight's Point.

She parked the car where Danny had, then walked up the Point to the statue, looking out across the blue sea where the sunshine danced and remembering how they'd walked along the beach below that day, hand in hand, in love and sure it would be forever. But it never is, of course. Nothing else is, why should love get special treatment?

She looked at the statue, and frowned. Something...

She ran her fingers over the near-blank face, to where the bump of the moustache should have been.

It wasn't there.

But as her fingers ran over the stone chin, she gasped as they encountered a narrow indentation in the rock, about two inches long. Almost like a scar.

She knew then, and weeping, she hugged herself tightly to the unyielding stone, her tears glistening on its shoulder.

After a while - how long she never knew, she lifted her head and touched the stone face one last time. And encountered a wetness, clear to look at and salty to taste, just below the rimmed outline of one eye.

She smiled a sweet, sad smile, and her walk back down the Point grew in strength in confidence, without a backward glance.

She got in the car, still smiling, and drove away.

It could have been a fleck of seawater, but she knew it wasn't. Even if the sea hadn't been as flat and calm as a millpond, she knew spume from a tear.

Old Lady Cat-Trash

Rain Graves and Mark McLaughlin

Old Lady Cat-Trash lived at the far, far end of a trailer park at the edge of Muddy Branch road in Smalls, Georgia. She had one of those fancy doublewides, with real gas heat *and* a nice electric generator that made some of the other folks a mite jealous 'round wintertime.

Of course, her name hadn't always been Cat-Trash, and she hadn't always been old. But she wasn't inclined to talk about her younger life. The only folks she ever talked to about anything were usually children – but they just ran from her as soon as she flashed her yellowy rotten-tooth smile.

She lived on a hill, with a lake on one side and the woods on the other. No one parked their trailers up on hills. To do so seemed a bit high-and-mighty, especially when she was probably the only one who could afford better if she wanted. Most trailer folks in them parts didn't have two nickels to rub together.

It didn't help knowing the Old Lady Cat-Trash took in stray felines, and was up to about twelve at the moment. On Halloween, the kids knew she'd be giving out the good candy because she could afford it. But still, most of them would take a good long hour just to get up the nerve to walk up the hill in the still, cold night, to knock on her rusty-screened door.

The trees have eyes tonight, tonight... So the old saying went. And Old Lady Cat-Trash's trees had several sets – about twelve – glittering gold and green from above, staring out from dark fur-edged silhouettes in the moonlight. You didn't see them much during the day. And the ones you did see...you pretended you didn't. They were all black, every one. No one liked them, and no one liked Old Lady Cat-Trash.

"You see all that damn garbage piling up, Mae Belle? Nothing but cat-food and tuna fish tins. I swear someone ought to go shoot up those damn cats of hers. Fry them up like a good catfish dinner. Ain't nothing good about 'em."

"That's just superstition talking," said Mae Belle.

"Ain't right, I tell you. Old hag like that got nothing to show the world but her piles and piles of trash. Why, there's so much trash heaped around her trailer, it smells worse than a shithouse at high noon. Can't even get close enough to look into her windows. Not that I'd wanna. Lord, she probably walks around naked with her old hag-titties hanging down to her knees."

"What a thing to say! Jessie, if you ain't got anything nice to say, don't say nothing at all. Cat-Trash is an old woman, and it ain't likely we'll see her carting them bags down that big hill. I don't think her old bones could take that kind of strain. She'd be in pain for days after all that."

"That's what beer's for," said Jessie, cracking open a can of Budweiser. "What you suppose she does up there all day? I only ever see her when she's off to the woods – Lord knows what business she has out there."

"Ain't none your business, Jess." Mae Belle shook her head, and lit a cigarette.

"Bet she's cooking up spells. I bet you she's got bat wings and eyeballs and whatnot all up her cupboards."

"You're crazy. You know that, don't you?"

"I bet you she's got Lily Beth's dead baby's *arm* up there in a fancy refriger-ate-in' unit! You know they never found that baby's arm? I can't believe they never found that baby's arm..."

"Jessica Louise Swanson, if I hadn't known you from when you were a child yourself, I'd slap you right across your crooked little face. You got no reason bringing Lily Beth's baby into this. That child drowned in the lake, and you know anything could've bitten that boy's arm off. Old Lady Cat-Trash has lived here long as I can remember – since I was a little girl myself – and we got no right to accuse her of such things. She's a harmless, lonely old woman, and her feline friends help her forget she's so miserable. That's all."

Jessie was silent, premature wrinkles creasing her forehead. She was thirty, but she'd been smoking since she was seven, so her face had a worn, leathery look. Maybe that was why she'd never found a husband – or rather, why one had never found her. She twirled a curl of bleached hair as she stared up the hill. Her eyes narrowed, and suddenly she looked triumphant.

"How old are you, Mae?"

"Sixty-seven. But I feel fifty," she grinned.

"And you've lived here how long?"

"All my life," Mae Belle said proudly. "This area's been my home since Mama died and Daddy left me as a baby to the Wickersons. They couldn't just let me lay, of course, and it was the Depression –"

"Never seen her young, *have* you, Mae?" Jessie's eyes glittered, finally having won the argument. When she saw Mae's face go a shade paler, she too felt a strange sort of shiver creep up her spine.

When Mae Belle spoke again, she spoke softly. "Reckon I never have."

Lily Beth walked up, and gave them a tragic sort of smile – the kind of smile that comes from losing something precious and never quite getting over it, but hating people fussing over you for it. It was a good fake smile. One she almost meant as real.

"Hey, Mae Belle. Hey, Jessie."

"Hey..." They said in unison.

"What you talking about?"

"Nothing," Mae Belle said.

"Weather's about to change," Lily said, staring at the backs of leaves shivering on trees, and the sudden smell of bark and dirt in the air.

"Hope it's not a late-season twister," Mae Belle said. "We always get one or two of them freak-of-nature things, just before October..." She turned to stare at Old Lady Cat-Trash's house. Jessie's words had got her to thinking. She thought about the missing arm of poor Lily's boy, and how they'd had to dredge the shallow end of the lake before they found his four-year-old body, bloated, all blue and pink like some kind of fancy bird feather.

They'd found the body jammed in some rocks, near a drop that went from waist-high to where you couldn't place your pole at the bottom. As a matter of fact, thought Mae Belle, the very spot was at the foot of Old Lady Cat-Trash's hill, clear on the other side. There *had* been claw marks and bites on the boy's shoulder and the arm that was left, as well as some pecks here and there on his stomach and side. Everyone figured the turkey vultures had gotten to him while he was floating on the surface – but none could figure out just what pulled him down under. Unless it was a gator. Folks called them waters a lake, but really, they were just the nicer end of a big old swamp. On some days, the wind would blow in a swamp-stench that would roll your eyes back in your head.

Mae thought she saw movement in the cat-lady's window. She thought she saw the outline of a head shaking back and forth, as if that old hag could hear her thoughts.

"I best be getting home. Hank will want a can of beans and weenies waiting when he goes hunting for his beer," Lily Beth said, laying a hand on Mae Belle's shoulder, causing her to jump. "Ain't you the twitchy one! What's got into you?"

"Nothing," Mae Belle lied, as she and Jessie exchanged a look.

That night, stretched out under some threadbare, yellowed sheets in her rickety bed, Mae Belle couldn't help but think more about what Jessie had said.

Yeah, Old Lady Cat-Trash had always been old. Always. Was that possible?

She sat up and looked out her window. She looked out at the trailer up on top of the hill, lights blazing – the cat-lady was still up. She glanced at her bedside clock with its glow-in-the-dark hands. Two-thirty. Well, didn't that beat all? She opened her nightstand drawer and pulled out her binoculars. She didn't have a TV– watching neighbors was pretty much the only show in town for her. She focused in on the Old Lady Cat-Trash residence.

Cats crawling around the trailer windows, and every now and then, a headful of scraggly hair popping into view, all in silhouette – nothing too out of the ordinary. Suddenly the scary old trailer woman lifted something, tossed it in the air and caught it. Jesus Christ Almighty, was that a baby? It sure as Hell looked like that old witch was tossing a baby up and down with glee, just as evil as you please.

Mae Belle's heart thumped in her throat like a kettledrum. What was she to do? She didn't have a phone, and her nearest neighbor– well, that was Old Lady Cat-Trash. By the time she found a phone at this hour, it would be too late – cat food, that's what that baby would be. Chopped up fine, or maybe mooshed up, like that fancy French meat paste some hoity-toity restaurants served up.

Mae Belle put on her shoes and coat, and then went to her kitchen and found a butcher knife. She'd stab the hag if she had to – the police would probably give her a medal for doing it. She felt a little dizzy, though. So much excitement couldn't be good for her heart.

She slipped out of her trailer and shuffled toward the hill, clenching the knife handle, praying she would have enough muscle to do what needed to be done. Some cats darted in front of her and she froze. Would they go tell the cat-lady she was coming? She'd once heard in a story, told by a teacher back when she was little, that witches had animal friends that helped with all them evil doings.

Why *did* some people do such bad things? she wondered. Maybe they'd been hurt once and they just had to hurt others. Still, Mae Belle's first husband Lamont used to slap her around, but that didn't make her want to go slapping anybody else. Maybe some people had bad parts in their brains, like some cars had bad parts and needed to get sent back to the factory. Or maybe... Well, she supposed there might be cases where doing a bad thing might make something good happen. Wasn't there some fancy French novel or movie or something about a guy getting into trouble for feeding his family with stolen bread...?

She slipped past some thorny bushes, but got too close – some pricklies snagged her coat and ripped it some. She shot a glance toward the trailer, hoping that the cat-lady hadn't heard. The old witch wasn't bouncing that baby any longer – was that good or bad? Mae Belle took a deep breath and ran right up to the trailer. The door was on the other side. Quiet as a little mouse, she snuck around the corner, around a big stack of garbage, and –

"Well, well, well! What have we here?" Old Lady Cat-Trash stood right in front of her, hands on hips. "Looks like a lady with a knife come to visit. You gonna kill me, Mae Belle? Frankly, I didn't take you for the murderin' type."

"Where's that baby?" Mae Belle screamed. "I saw you in your window, tossing a baby up and down." She raised the knife. "You just hand over that little precious or I'll – well, I'll just have to kill you."

The cat-lady cackled like a broody hen. "Thank you, Mae Belle, for the laugh-riot of this here century. You're funnier than one of them Martin and Lewis movies they don't make no more. Yeah, I've got that baby, right here." She turned, marched to her door and reached over the threshold. She then marched back and shoved a big cloth baby-doll in her face. "Save the baby, Mae Belle, before I make it into a dish rag! I swear, this is going in my diary! Oh, this is *rich!*"

"I am so sorry, I just saw what I saw and let my imagination get the best of me! Please forgive me –" She dropped the knife. "I was gonna call you by name, but I'm not sure I'm remembering it right. Sally? No... Sarah, isn't it? Forgive me, Sarah."

Old Lady Cat-Trash cocked her head to one side. "Well, I'll be fried. There's still one soul in this town who remembers my name. Yes, it's Sarah. Short for Sarracenia. Come in the trailer, sugar. Brave old bitch like you deserves a swig of my finest brandy."

Mae Belle put her hands to her cheeks. "Brandy! That's what rich people drink."

The cat-lady guffawed. "Well, I ain't poor. I gotta warn you, though, the place needs a little tidying up." She entered the trailer and Mae Belle followed.

The reek of feline piss and poop just about knocked her on her ass. Sarah noticed her distress. "Yeah, I guess gets a little whiffy in here," she said. "I don't notice it too much, though." The trailer was filled with boxes, magazines, newspapers, cloth dolls and sacks of garbage. The scraggly-haired woman rummaged around until she'd found two glasses. Then she found a pretty crystal bottle and poured some equally pretty amber booze for the both of them. "Here ya go, sugar. This'll numb your nose-hairs so the stink don't gag ya too much."

Mae Belle waited until Sarah had taken a swig before she had one herself. My, but it went down smooth. "You mentioned your real name – it was all long and fancy. Is that French or something? I think French stuff is so *interesting*."

Sarah flashed her crappy teeth in a smile. "Yeah, them Frenchies got all kinds of class. Sarracenia is my name, and the name of a plant that eats bugs. My mother was an honest-and-for-true scientist, at a time when ladies didn't do that sort of thing. She had a head full of brains.

Let me freshen your drinky-poo there, sugar. You sure are one coura-geous bitch, coming up here with a knife, getting all ready to save some baby, just like we were in a Hollywood movie or something."

"But why would your mother name you after some monster plant? That don't make no sense." The drink was making Mae Belle feel light-headed.

"My mother used to say, 'A woman with a brain is like a flower with teeth.' She gave me that name so I'd always know that." She squeezed Mae Belle's forearm. "Say, you got some muscle on you. You wanna be my maid? I'll pay you fifty bucks a week."

Mae Belle gasped. "Fifty whole dollars a week?"

"Sure. I can't lift nothing on account of I have a bad back, just like my mother. Pinched nerves and everything. I got parts on my body I can't even feel. You don't have to clean everything up at once. A little patch here, little patch there."

Mae Belle looked around the trailer. Lord, but there was a lot of work to be done. But then, that was a good thing, wasn't it? A steady paycheck. The litterbox alone would probably take a week. It was about two feet deep, three feet wide and four feet long. Why in the world did she even *have* a catbox, when her trailer was right next to the woods? A cat can shit in the woods just as easily as a bear. "Sure, I'd be happy to do some cleanin' for ya. Of course, you'll give me a few bucks every now and then for cleaning supplies, right? Scrub brushes, soap, rubber gloves."

"Why, sure!"Sarah poured her an extra dollop of booze. "Scrub brushes! Glad to hear you're planning to put a little elbow grease into this old dump."

A striped yellow kitten climbed out of a pile of old papers and skipped right into the litterbox to take a poop. A moment later, another kitten, a black one, followed his pal into the crapper. Well, that ex-plained the indoor shitter. A kitten in the woods would get snatched up by some mean old critter, pronto. And old Sarah would still need a box big enough for the others, so the kittens could learn by watching their mommies do their business.

"I'd better be gettin' home," Mae Belle said. "Sorry about the mix-up – comin' to kill ya and all. And thanks for the job. What time should I get here tomorrow to get started?"

"Huzzah, got me a real eager beaver! I like sleepin' late, so noon'll be fine. You don't have to do a full eight hours a day, ya know. This ain't no factory. Four or five hours, that'll be fine. Still better than the zero I've been putting into the place!" Sarah reached down into her cleavage and pulled out some money. "Here's two twenties for you to buy some clean-ing supplies with. You don't got a car, do you? Maybe that gal you hang out with can drive you to the store."

Mae Belle nodded. "Oh, yeah, Jessie would be pleased to help. Her and me, we'd do anything for each other. We're like sisters that way."

"Well, maybe you and me'll be friends like that, someday. I'd like that. I said it before and I'll say it again – you're one brave old bitch!"

Woozy from the brandy, Mae Belle staggered back through the grass, through the trees, to her own home. Old Lady Cat-Trash wasn't so bad after all. She looked around her much smaller trailer. With that money, she could really pretty up the place. Maybe she'd even get a poster of one of them male dancers with the big muscle chests and little bow-ties. Them pretty boys usually liked other boys, but so what? Still easy on the eyes. A sight like that might give her some of them sexy dreams. Been a while since she had one of those. She sighed as she settled back in her bed. She used to have her own pretty boy, once upon a time. And he liked her just fine. He had a big chest, too. But he also had a big car that he liked driving really fast, and one day he ran right into a train. A man's got to be a little stupid, to run into something that big.

How she loved that stupid man. His name was Hap. She used to call him Happy-Hap-Hap, and that always made him laugh.

"I love you, Happy-Hap-Hap," she whispered, half-hoping she'd hear that big, dumb laugh of his in reply. But all she heard was one of Sarah's cats, mowling off in the distance.

The next morning around nine, Jessie stopped by and was dumbfounded by Mae Belle's account of her visit to Old Lady Cat-Trash.

"Well, I'll be poked and prodded," Jessie said. "She pulled forty bucks right out of her titty-sling? Hope you washed her boob-lice off them bills."

"Listen to you! You must think you're one of them Hollywood stand-up comics. We'll better get to the store right now and buy some cleaning supplies, so we'll be back by noon." Mae Belle looked over a shopping list she'd prepared. "Lemon juice gets the stink out of things, right? I'd better pick up a *lot* of lemon juice. Cheaper than them fancy air fresheners. Those sprays would probably be no good for her cats anyway."

"So she's really okay?" Jessie asked, obviously still a little leery. "She didn't try to put no spells on you, did she? Was she talkin' backwards at any point in time? Backwards talkin' is a sure sign of evil."

Mae Belle rolled her eyes. "Just get me to the store. That junk car of yours has more devil in it than anything else in Georgia."

Jessie nodded. "Yeah, we don't want her firing you on the first day. Forty bucks! That's a sweet chunk of change. Can't say I blame ya for accepting her offer. Why, if old Mr. Devil pulled forty bucks out of his jockstrap for me, I'd go sweep the floors in Hell and maybe even clean the toilets, too."

At noon, when Mae Belle walked up to Sarah's trailer, she found a note taped to the door. Sarah had really pretty handwriting, all loopy and curly.

Mae - Let yourself in, hon. I'll be in the woods picking mushrooms. Just like an evil old witch, hee hee heee! I'll make us a nice mushroom soup when I get home. Don't worry, I've been eating it for years and it ain't killed me yet! - Sarah

So that was what Sarah did in the woods. Picked mushrooms. Probably berries, too. The door wasn't locked. Of course, everyone was afraid of Old Lady Cat-Trash, so no one was about to go barging inside. Yep, fear probably worked a lot better than any chintzy lock for keeping folks out. Mae Belle carried two plastic bags full of cleaning products into the trailer and dumped them on the floor, scaring the cats.

Her first duty, she decided, what to attack that stink-pot of a litterbox. She'd bought a nice little slotted plastic shovel for the occasion, and plenty of trashbags, too. She put on some rubber gloves and got to work. The sooner she started the job, the sooner it'd be done.

"Scoop, scoop, scoop. Scoop the poop..." She sang a little song as she worked. Happy-Hap-Hap used to love her little songs. Yeah, he was stupid - smart guys don't go driving into trains - but he loved everything little thing about her.

The black kitten crept up and added a fresh little burden to her workload. "Trying to give me some job security, little man?" she said. "Ain't you considerate. I'm gonna call you Happy-Hap-Hap. How's that sound?"

Mae Belle continued to scoop and dump, scoop and scoop, until she'd filled a plastic bag a third full. It was getting pretty heavy, what with so many cat-rocks in it, so she tied it off, then folded the excess bag around the bulk of it and tied it off again. There. A nice tidy bundle. She reached for a fresh bag and began scooping again. She plunged her little shovel under another longish rounded lump, shook away the grit, and suddenly realized that she was looking at -

A bone. Two bones, actually, jointed in the middle. If she didn't know better, she'd have sworn it looked like part of...a finger...

But no. Couldn't be. Some cat must've dragged part of some dead bird or possum in the grit. She looked at the bones, all dead and creepy in the middle of her shovel. Finally she reached into the shovel, picked them up and -

- *Found herself in the cold, on an outcropping of rock overlooking a big dark canyon. But then, maybe it wasn't a canyon. Canyons weren't filled with red and green-yellow stars that swirled slow, leaving trails of oily light. Canyons didn't have horrible shapes as big as houses grunting and howling and milling around way down below. Not canyons on Earth anyway. One of the stars floated toward her and she saw that it was really - Oh Lord - some sort of glowing jelly-*

fish, sucking in air and moving by puffing the air out again. One of the shapes below shifted and lunged up on top of another shape. Then it lunged against the wall of the canyon immediately below her. It was trying to climb up to her. Trying to get her. It was hard to think - her head felt like it was filled with old frying pan oil, all thick and filthy with old burnt meat - but she tried to remember how she'd gotten to this freezing corner of hell, and she remembered a couple old bones. Bones she was still holding. She thought real hard and tried to remember how to open her fingers and -

- She was back in the trailer, lying in the middle of that damned catbox, surrounded by kittens looking at her all curious. She scrambled out of the litter and managed to get back on her feet. She steadied herself against a wall, her heart racing a million miles an hour.

In the litter, instead of those bones, she saw a small, shiny lump of -

Gold.

By God, yes! It was only about as big as a vitamin pill, but it was gold all right. The sight of that tiny treasure drove all the fear right out of her brain. Never mind that she'd just looked down into the bowels of Hell itself - she had a piece of gold now! She looked around. She was still alone - old Sarah was probably still off in the woods. She snatched up the nugget and stuck it in one of her pockets. For a frantic moment she wondered what to do next...

Quick as her feet could carry her, she ran home, hid her little treasure under the sink, and then ran back to Sarah's again. She still had a lot of cleaning to do. But not in that litterbox.

She still had to think about *that.*

Later, Sarah came back and made her some mushroom soup. And it was delicious.

A week passed.

Mae Belle continued cleaning for Sarah and of course, didn't dare mention the gold. She didn't make any attempt to sell it. Truth to tell, she wasn't sure how to go about such a thing. A big-city place would probably want some kind of explanation of how she'd gotten it. Or would they?

Finally, she decided: if she found any more gold, she'd just keep collecting it until she had a nice little stack. Then her and Jessie would just get in the car and drive to some city and take it from there. If her and Jessie put their heads together, they'd be able to figure out how to sell that gold. Maybe they could say it had been in one of their families for a long time. That might work. Oh yes, it was time to sell an old family treasure.

Once, she had a bright idea and asked Jessie to buy her a nice raw steak - one with a bone in it - at the store. Then, while Sarah was out in the woods, she flopped the steak into the catbox and stood back. She felt guilty, tossing a nice piece of meat into a shitpile, but she figured it was what you'd call an *investment*.

Nothing happened.

Then she remembered that she'd had her *hands* on that little bone.

So she reached down, grabbed the steak and –

– Again she was out in the cold, on the rock, staring into the dark canyon. And it was clear that she had done something very wrong. The jellyfish puffed and swirled all furious and crazy around her, and the shapes down below roared like thunder, shifting and throwing themselves up against the rock walls. One jumped so high that she was able to see the nightmare that passed for its face. It looked like a gigantic asshole surrounded with hot yellow eyes and hundreds of flappy ribbons of skin. Frantic, she opened her hand and –

She was back in the trailer, facedown in the cat litter. She pulled herself to her feet, brushed the grit off of her and looked to see what they'd left for her.

It wasn't gold.

It looked like a sausage-sized maggot that had been boiled in tar. The horrible thing was still alive, too – barely. It uttered a high squeal and thick ooze began to gush out of little holes in its sides. Thankfully, a big tomcat came along and carried the horrible thing away.

One later afternoon, while she was scrubbing Sarah's floor, she happened to notice some brown spots by the wall. When she rubbed at them, the soapy froth came up all reddish.

She looked over to Sarah, who was all wrapped up in the book she was reading in the doorway of the big trailer.

Without a word, Mae Belle finished cleaning up the old bloodstain and then moved on to some other stains that weren't so scary.

"You are doing one fine job. You know that?" Sarah said. "This place is starting to smell like pine trees and lemons instead of cat pee. I guess I was so used to that stink it didn't really register. Well, you know what they say. A person can get used to anything. In time."

Mae Belle sighed. "Yes. I suppose so."

Sarah fetched the brandy bottle and poured each of them a swig.

"Thanks kindly," Mae Belle said.

Sarah looked at her fondly. "Like I said when we first met. You really are a brave old bitch. Imagine the likes of you meeting the Dwellers on their turf – and not even saying one word about it, like it was some kind of everyday happening."

Mae Belle swallowed her drink in one chug. "Hellfire. Is that what those things are called? Dwellers? How'd you even find out about that?"

The old cat-lady smirked. "Honey, I've been doing business with the Dwellers for a right long time. I gots me a way of getting in touch with their minds. They let me know somebody new has been to see them

- twice. Well, I don't need to be no Einstein to figure out it was you. Oh, and you can keep that gold they gave ya. Call it a tip, like them big-city waitresses get. More brandy?"

Mae Belle only nodded.

"The truth is, honey," Sarah said, pouring more brandy for her helper, "is that there are some spots on this old Earth that are more - special - than others. One is right under that god-damned litterbox. It's my bank, so I can never leave here. The other is out in them woods. That's where I do my business. How would you like to help me make a big transaction? It's too big to do myself."

Even though she was drinking, Mae Belle's throat felt as dry as an an old gritty cat-turd. "I'm listening," she rasped. "What will I get out of this thing we ... might do?"

"If you help me with this one task," Sarah said, "I will give you enough money to last the rest of your life. I can just hand it to ya when we're done - I have it stashed away here in the trailer. Enough to get you out of this shit-hole trailer park and set you up somewhere right fancy. Maybe that old France you like so much. It's a sweet deal. All you've gotta do is say 'Yes'."

Mae Belle breathed deeply for a minute, thinking. France. Fancy-pants France would be so nice, so truly nice, after long hard years of just getting by. "Sure. I don't have nothing to lose. If I die trying, well - I'm old anyway. Jessie would miss me, but that's about it. What do I have to do?"

Sarah took her hand. "Just come with me and follow instructions. That's all."

The two old women walked into the woods.

It was starting to get dark, but Mae Belle tried not to let this worry her. She had never been in this part of the woods before. The trees here seemed bigger, with coarser bark and thick branches that were way too twisty for her liking.

Sarah led her to a huge black rock spotted with a white, slimy fungus. "Put your hand on the rock," she said, "and then your lips." Mae Belle did as she was told and -

- *Rushed at a dizzying speed, through swarms of thick, furry worms and things that looked like wasps made out of dirty glass, through hallways of flames and screams, through crazy-ass mirrors filled with wiggly-angly shapes that keep growing and dividing and feeding on each other, on and on, faster and faster, until she reached -*

- Another black rock, between two dead trees in the middle of some thick bushes.

"The problem is," Sarah said, leading Mae Belle through the bushes, "I can't carry much. My mother had a bad back too, ya know - I used to help her, just like you're helping me now."

When they emerged from the bushes, they were in a run-down park in a city slum, just outside an alleyway. Here it was the middle of the night, with stars overhead and garbage all over the place. Sarah led the way into the alley and continued talking.

"Oh, she was a smart one. She's the one who discovered the passageways and how to find them – tunnels through space, sometimes even dimensions. She introduced me to the Dwellers, too. Dead human meat or bone, *hand-delivered!* That's the only thing that makes *them* happy. Gold isn't their only reward. They can give great pleasure, too. Not the big ones, of course. They'd squish a person. I know how to summon the smaller ones – they can be so gentle, and they have parts of them...you just can't imagine. That's my favorite part – the gold's just icing on the cake. The more meat I bring, the more they reward me. Problem is, I can only carry them a few small pieces every now and then. That why I need you: to make a big haul. One that'll last me for a spell."

"Did you kill Lily Beth's baby?" Mae Belle said. "I can't –"

"There you go again with babies!" Sarah said with a laugh. "No, but I did find it in the water. Don't know how it got there. Maybe the daddy never wanted her to *have* that kid. But I didn't want the Dwellers to develop a real *taste* for baby, so I just took them an arm. Just a little piece to hold them over at the time." The she put a finger to her lips. "I'd better quiet down," she whispered. "Time for business."

They'd come across a big cardboard box on its side. A water-warped, duct-taped refrigerator box, with a candle or lamp of some sort flickering inside. Sarah reached into her ample cleavage and pulled out a folded hunting knife. Lord, Mae Belle thought, what else does she have tucked away around her old boobies?

Sarah then unfolded the blade, and Mae Belle noticed that the cat-lady obviously hadn't cleaned it since the last time she'd used it.

"Who's out there?" asked a weak, trembling voice. An old man, or maybe some poor gal who'd smoked for fifty or sixty years.

"Social worker, sweety," Sarah said cheerfully, "inviting you to dinner."

"You can't fool me," the voice said. "You're the Alley Witch. I've heard about you, cutting parts off folks. Stay away. I've got a cross."

Sarah laughed and shook her head. "Good thing I ain't no Lady Dracula! You wait out here, Mae. Won't take more than a minute. Then you've got some carryin' to do."

The cat-lady then bent to enter the box, knife in hand. Suddenly an old man stormed out, swinging a crowbar. Sarah screamed as it came down on the back of her neck. She stumbled forward, pushing the man to the ground. His weapon flew off into the shadows.

The filthy old man, pinned under the dead cat-lady, looked toward Mae Belle, his eyes wide with fear. Quickly, she scooped up the knife from where Sarah dropped it.

"I don't have nothing against you, mister," she said. "But I've gotta look after myself, 'cause nobody else will." And then she stabbed him in the throat. Sick old bastard, he probably didn't have too long to live anyway.

It took over an hour, but she managed to drag both bodies back to the black rock in the park without anyone seeing her.

The next part was a little more complicated. First she took Sarah's dead hand as she touched and kissed the black rock. It wasn't too hard dragging her dead body through that crazy zone, since they were mostly floating anyway. Then she had to go back and get that dead tramp. At last she had them both transported to the woods.

She sighed wearily. She was bone-tired, and dragging both bodies back to the trailer through all those trees seemed like an impossible task that would take forever. Yeah, sure, she could cut them in smaller chunks. But even then she'd have to make a whole lot of trips. Sarah was a big gal.

Maybe she'd need some help.

Jessie looked out the window of the airplane. "Lord, girl. I can't believe we're on our way to Paris. First thing to do when we get there is to get us some of that bubbly French champagne."

"Yes, why not?" Mae Belle said. "We deserve it. We had to do a Hell of a lot of work."

Jessie bit her lower lip fretfully. "Let's not ever talk about that."

"That suits me just fine." Mae Belle sat up in her seat. "Oh, look. There's that nice Stuart feller. Look at the muscles on him. He looks so clean and he's got all his teeth, too."

"That ain't his name, ya know. It's his job. A steward is one of them male stewardesses." Jessie playfully poked her friend in the ribs. "You're old enough to be his grandma! Besides, he's so damn pretty, he's probably one of them boys who likes other boys."

Mae Belle shrugged. "I suppose. But he sure is easy on the eyes."

BIOGRAPHIES

Hugh Lamb is one of the most respected editors and anthologists in the genre. His numerous books such as A Tide Of Terror, Victorian Tales Of Terror, and The Taste Of Fear, introduced rare and forgotten stories to the present day reader. He provided stories for Enigmatic Tales, and edits books for Ash Tree Press as well as working as a free-lance proofreader; He is a giant in the field of supernatural fiction.

Kurt Newton has had over 200 stories and poems published in anthologies and magazines, receiving six Honourable Mentions along the way. His collection from Delirium, The House Spider and other strange visitors has been well received, as have his three poetry chapbooks. Kurt is also editor and publisher, and working on a novel or two.

Walt Jarvis lives in Los Angeles where he has written for both trade and consumer magazines. He has had short fiction published in several publications, most notably in "Enigmatic Tales" and in the anthology Bell, Book and Beyond.

Kim Guilbeau is a 26 year-old writer living in New England with her husband. More of her short stories have appeared in the anthologies Cemetery Sonata II and The Witching Hour along with many other small press magazines in print and on the net. She is hard at work on her first novel. Visit her on the web at www.redrival.com/kim

John Shire is a talented UK writer whose style is varied and innovative. He has seen a number of his stories published in a variety of magazines.

Roger Morris has written a larger collection Grimmer Tales from which this traditionally themed fable is taken. The Devil's Drum has been adapted as a music theatre piece by the composer Edward Dudley Hughes and was performed in the Purcell Room on the South Bank in

London by a group called Solaris. He has been published in various mainstream magazines and has written two novels.

Michael Laimo's first novel "Atmosphere" is forthcoming in paperback in early 2002 from Leisure Books. He has a hardcover collection out from Delirium Books, "Demons, Freaks, and Other Abnormalities", and two chapbooks, "Within the Darkness, Golden Eyes" from Flesh and Blood Press, and "The Twilight Garden" from Miranda-Jahya. He's appeared in over 100 anthologies and magazines. Look for another collection entitled "The Dregs Of Society" in 2001, both in Limited Edition hardcover and trade paperback, from Imaginary Worlds. He serves as associate editor for Space & Time Magazine, and fiction editor for Bloodtype, a hardcore horror anthology from Lone Wolf Publications. His website is at www.laimo.com E-mail: Michael@Laimo.com

Jack Fisher has (or will have) over 75 short works in print in such magazines as Dark Regions, Indigenous Fiction, Black October, Writer Online, Space & Time, Transversions, The Fractal, Reality's Escape, E-Scape, and more. He is the editor of Flesh & Blood magazine, which won the Jobs in Hell 2000 Year's Best Magazine Award. Jack is an EMT in Paramedic training.

Barbara Malenky lives and writes in Parker, Texas. Her non-fiction work has appeared in national crime magazines and paperback anthologies. Her fiction has appeared in over 300 magazines including Pirate Writings, Space and Time and the anthology Year One. She received an honourable mention in the Year's Best Fantasy and Horror Twelfth Annual Collection for her short story "Seasons". Her chap- book, Human Oddities, is available from www.deliriumbooks.com She is currently working on her first novel.

Michelle Scalise has sold close to two hundred poems and short stories to such magazines as The Urbanite, Carpe Noctem, Dark Regions, Talebones, Roadworks and such anthologies as Dark Side 2, Viscera, Die Drachen Von Morgen, Bell Book And Beyond and Women's Best Erotica 2001.

Stefano Donati has published some sixty short stories and in 1998 won an L. Ron Hubbard Award for best short story by a new writer. He has also earned an Honorable Mention in Year's Best Fantasy & Horror for his alternate biography of Myra Hindley. He lives in Vermont, USA and is a huge fan of many British musicians and writers.

Beth Lewis is a 14 (yes - fourteen) year old English girl who writes fantasy and horror as if she was born to it. A poem has recently won a local competition and a synopsis and sample chapters of a fantasy novel are currently under consideration. Her short stories combine grace, fear and artistic flair. What will she achieve at 15?

Richard Gavin has published numerous short stories and poems, all in the horror/dark fantasy vein. His writings have appeared in Canada, the United States, England and France. A member of the Horror Writers Association, Richard lives in Ontario, Canada, where he is at work on a new novel.

Lynda E. Rucker lives in Portland, Oregon, USA and travels as much as she can afford (and she's met several of the occupants of the Seagull Hostel along the way). She's had stories published in The Third Alternative, recently completed her first novel, and is at work on a second one.

Donald Murphy was born in Denver and has a degree in literature from Colorado State University. He currently lives in Madrid, where he teaches English and works as a freelance translator. His stories, with their exotic locations and fantastic themes, have recently been popping up in publications in both the US and Europe, a fact which his wife finds greatly relieving. His first published story, "El Chivo", appeared last year in Enigmatic Tales Electronic.

Alison L R Davies is a writer of both poetry and prose from Nottingham. I have four collections of poetry published, my most recent a collection entitled 'Beyond the Fey'. My horror stories range from Psychological to Supernatural. I am currently working on a collection for publication some time later this year. I have been published in 'The Dark Fantasy Newsletter', 'Unhinged', 'Dark Horizons', 'Scribe', and an American magazine entitled 'Gaslight' has recently accepted me. My work is also appearing in a web showcase called 'DarkMoon'. In my spare time I enjoy horse-riding, tarot reading and listening to spooky music! My web site address is www.alisonlrdavies.co.uk

Simon Bestwick is an English writer whose work has appeared in numerous magazines and anthologies. He has been the editor of the Oktobyr series of anthologies and his work has attracted Honourable Mentions.

Mark McLaughlin/Rain Graves. Mark is a writer of fiction and poetry that has appeared in over 250 publications. His work has appeared in chapbooks that have been published that have been published widely in USA. He is the editor of the successful The Urbanite. Rain is a Californian writer whose work has been published in a variety of magazines and anthologies. She was the featured poet in Urbanite 11 and is the poetry editor at Gothic.Net.

Iain Maynard is a talented UK artist who has also seen his stories published in magazines. His artwork has graced a number of magazines and anthologies, and can be seen on the covers of the hardback collection Echoes Of Darkness.

Len Maynard & Mick Sims, www.maynard-sims.com, are writers as well as editors, and have been publishers (Enigmatic Press). Numerous stories have been published in magazines and anthologies in UK and USA, attracting award nominations and Honourable Mentions. Moths, their Honourable Mentioned novella is out from Cosmos Books, and in addition two collections of their stories, essays and interviews featuring work never before published in USA are due from Cosmos Books in the Summer as a two volume set, each containing 100,000 words - The Secret Geography Of Nightmare and Selling Dark Miracles. They co-edit F20 with David Howe for The British Fantasy Society. Their third hardback collection of supernatural stories, Incantations - following Shadows At Midnight and the Stoker recommended Echoes Of Darkness - has been accepted by Imaginary Worlds. A standalone novella, The Business Of Barbarians, is completed, and awaiting acceptance. Another standalone novella, The Hidden Language Of Demons, has been accepted by Imaginary Worlds. A young adult novel, The Seminar has been completed.

www.ingramcontent.com/pod-product-compliance
Lightning Source LLC
Chambersburg PA
CBHW051843170626
46807CB00003B/1329